D1084741

SILENT HEART

SILENT HEART

•

KATHY ATTALLA

AVALON BOOKS
THOMAS BOUREGY AND COMPANY, INC.
401 LAFAYETTE STREET
NEW YORK, NEW YORK 10003

PRINTED IN THE UNITED STATES OF AMERICA
ON ACID-FREE PAPER
BY HADDON CRAFTSMEN, BLOOMSBURG, PENNSYLVANIA

To my family, for accepting if not understanding my obsession with writing. A special thanks to my critique partners Janet, Renee, Bette, and especially Karen for not complaining when she read all five rewrites of my story.

Chapter One

Luke Clayborne's gaze followed the long seams of the black lace stockings until they disappeared under the hem of a red miniskirt. He stuffed the crumpled invitation into his pocket and leaned back against the wall of the gymnasium with a groan. If he was the human computer his cousin accused him of being, his hard drive had just kicked into turbo speed. He tipped back the Styrofoam cup and took a large gulp of the punch that a student had pushed into his hand upon his arrival. The fruity liquid did little to cool his interest.

He returned his attention to the only person in the room to pique his curiosity so far this evening. To his disappointment, her skirt was topped off by a baggy white, man's-style shirt, bloused at the waist with a wide canvas belt. Red crew socks and sneakers completed the rather unusual outfit. *Who is she?* he wondered. She was too old to be a student and far too unorthodox to be a faculty member at the Kennelworth Institute for the Deaf. He guessed that like him, she was related to one of the graduating seniors.

She pushed a handful of chestnut ringlets behind her ear and continued with her conversation. Her delicate hands moved in a rapid succession of gestures. A group of captivated teenagers watched and smiled. Occasionally a nervous laugh carried above the unintelligible murmurs in the room. He wished now that he had found the time to learn Sign Language as his mother and Robert had begged him to do. He had meant to, but business and perhaps his own fears had kept him from taking that first step.

"Put your eyes back in your head."

Luke turned toward his smirking cousin. "Who is she, Robert?"

Robert's smile faded. "Don't you know?"

"Should I?"

"Yes, you should. She's all Kyle talks about, but then, you can't even understand your own sister, so why should you know about anyone who matters to her?"

Luke winced. That arrow had hit a bull's-eye. He recognized the tight constriction in his chest as guilt. That same guilt that had been quietly nagging him since he had agreed to attend the graduation party for his younger sister. How had she grown up without him realizing it? He thought he'd have more time. Boarding school was over and she would be home for good now.

His cousin was right. He couldn't do more than pass notes across a table and in the last two years, Kyle hadn't bothered to answer those. If he needed any more proof of the chasm between them, he need only look around the party. Kyle was conspicuous by her absence. The minute she had seen him, she had left with a group of her friends.

"... teacher," Robert said.

"Excuse me?"

"Jade Allenwood. She's one of Kyle's teachers. You must have heard your mother talk about her?"

Luke felt another blast of guilt. He gave his mother the same deaf ear that Kyle gave him. Only Kyle had a better excuse.

Again, he sought out Jade Allenwood. He couldn't recall having a teacher who looked quite like her when he was back in high school. "What does she teach?"

"Why don't you ask her?" Robert's question held a challenge Luke decided to accept.

"I will."

"Wait," Robert called out, but Luke had already started across the room. The small audience that had surrounded Ms. Allenwood earlier had broken up and she stood alone.

"Miss Allenwood. Could I have a word with you?"

Without so much as a turn in his direction, she walked away. That Robert witnessed the way she had ignored him only added to his embarrassment. Although Luke hadn't expected her to fall all over him just because he made substantial donations to the school, he did expect a little courtesy from someone who earned a living from the institution.

"What happened, Luke?"

"You know exactly what happened. I suppose you knew it would. Has she done the same to you?"

Robert smiled. "Never. Actually I have a rather friendly relationship with her. She's been the only person who could consistently get through to Kyle and keep her out of trouble."

Robert raised his hand and gestured toward one of the students. They made an exchange of signs. Suddenly, Jade appeared from seemingly nowhere. She walked toward them, flashing a brilliant smile in Robert's direction.

"Look at her when you speak, even if you're talking to me," Robert said. "She lip-reads."

"She's deaf?" Relief washed over him, soothing his bruised ego. "I thought she was ignoring me."

Jade stopped directly in front of them. She signed with her hands and once again, he silently cursed himself for not making the time to learn this language of the deaf. He waited for his cousin to stop laughing so Robert could translate.

"She said she *was* ignoring you, Luke."

A peculiar frown crossed her face as they were introduced. Eyes, a vivid shade of green that matched her name, narrowed as she continued her dialogue with Robert.

"Why doesn't Luke answer for himself?" Robert translated. His cousin's smirk mocked him.

"I don't understand Sign." Luke's simple admission brought a glare of scorn. And then, as if to prove him wrong, she shot her hands up in disgust, a gesture so clearly expressing her anger that he couldn't fail to understand.

"Do you need that interpreted?" Robert asked as they watched her storm across the room.

Luke laughed. "No. I got it."

"I hope you're still amused on Monday."

"Why?"

"She's got an interview at Direct Mail for a summer job, only she doesn't know you own the company."

Luke paused and assessed the temperament of the green-eyed beauty. "Somehow, Robert, I don't think she would have done anything differently had she known."

Jade slouched into a chair in the ladies' locker room and tried to get her temper under control. It never failed to infuriate her when a family member refused to learn Sign. Although she spoke quite well, she made no effort for a person who clearly didn't think that communicating in her language was worth the effort either.

Kyle had mentioned her older brother on several occasions, but in the three years since Jade had been teaching at the Kennelworth Institute, Lucas Clayborne had not attended one school function with the rest of his family. Did he think his sister would forgive him for the years of silence?

As a student advisor as well as a business teacher, Jade had found Kyle her biggest challenge. The bright and talented young woman carried a chip on her shoulder the size of Plymouth Rock. More than once, Jade had risen to Kyle's defense, recognizing her rebellious streak as a cry for attention to a man who chose not to hear. She couldn't help but worry what would happen once Kyle returned home for good.

After splashing cold water on her face, Jade went back out to join the party. She ducked under a crepe-paper streamer that had begun to droop. Mr. Stanton, the dean and her boss, shot her an angry scowl and waved her over. Great! She knew she should have kept her opinions and gestures to herself but sometimes her hands got ahead of her brain.

"Jade. What were you thinking?"

She pointed to her temple and feigned temporary insanity.

Dean Stanton shook his finger in front of her face. "Don't you play innocent with me. That man is one of our most generous patrons."

"If he understood me," she signed, "then it's the only thing he understood all evening."

The older man tried unsuccessfully to hide his amused grin behind a stern veneer. Stanton was her strongest supporter. Jade's unwavering obsession with teaching her students total self-reliance upset some of the very parents who wanted the best for their children. She never accepted deafness as a handicap to her students or herself. The deaf community had much to offer, but she didn't believe in shutting out the rest of the world—a position that was often unpopular among some of her professors at Gallaudet University.

"You're lucky Mr. Clayborne has a good sense of humor, but you still owe him an apology."

She shook her head and stomped her foot to stress her disagreement. "He owes his sister an apology."

"Listen." He grabbed her hands before she could sign again. "You teach your students . . . no, you insist they don't cut themselves off from the hearing world. For Kyle Clayborne that world includes her brother. You have no right to judge a situation knowing only one side. So, if you aren't going to apologize, then stay away from him for the rest of the evening."

"My pleasure," she signed defiantly.

He chuckled. "Your pleasure would be to follow up with a few gestures known mostly to taxi drivers and drunken sailors. If you can't behave, then slide your hands in your pockets and shut up."

"Anything else?"

"Yes. About your clothes. Is that what you call appropriate?"

Jade closed her eyes to cut him off. Her outfit had been a deliberate rebellion against a mandate she found unacceptable. She had been requested to dress "appropriately" and make a good impression on the male patrons. No one told James Hurley, the shop teacher, to dress in a tux and pay court to the wealthy widows. She understood that no institution ran without money but she refused to be dangled as bait for a school of lecherous sharks.

Stanton touched her arm and she opened her eyes.

"You're a good teacher, Jade, but one day that temper of yours is going to land you in trouble and I won't be able to bail you out. I'm not sure who you are so angry with, but don't make the mistake of transferring that anger to Luke Clayborne. Sometimes you can do more harm than good in defending your students."

Stanton left her alone to think about his warning. She reached for a cup of punch and retreated to a vacant corner. Students passed and she raised her cup in a silent toast. Lord, she hated graduation day. She always felt like she was losing a friend. Perhaps that would explain her irrational behavior this evening.

She had to admit, though not without a fair amount of denial, that she might be transferring her anger with her own brother to Luke Clayborne. After all, she'd met many men in the past few years who had been unable or unwilling to master more than the basics of American Sign Language. Why did she feel such resentment toward Kyle's brother? And why did she care? After today she probably wouldn't be seeing either of them again. A sadness washed over her.

Deciding to take the least emotional course, she

tossed her cup in the garbage and headed out the exit doors. She couldn't afford to get nostalgic now. A long summer awaited her, and if the job lead Robert had given her didn't work out, she had to find something quickly.

She was so close to reaching her goal and this summer's earnings could put her over the top. Although the doctor had warned her the new procedure had only a thirty-percent success rate in cases like hers, she felt the short odds were better than none at all. Unfortunately, her insurance company didn't agree, so she would have to pay for the experimental surgery herself.

Jade sat in the lobby and fidgeted with the edge of the employment application. Where was Robert? He said he would meet her at one o'clock. She couldn't stall much longer. The receptionist would think she was a brainless idiot, unable to fill out a simple form in less than half an hour.

Her stubborn courage was rapidly deserting her. Although the temporary job as a data entry clerk didn't require hearing as a prerequisite, many prospective employers had tactfully yet quickly dismissed her without consideration when they realized she was deaf. Robert assured her that the boss wouldn't care, but to put her mind at ease, he had promised to make a personal introduction. She glanced at her watch. She would have to make it through the interview alone.

Taking a deep breath, she stood up and brought the application to the receptionist. The young woman lowered her head and spoke while attempting to read over the application. Jade tried to make out as many words as possible but she hadn't caught enough to know she was suppose to return to the lobby, until the annoyed woman raised her head and repeated the words.

So much for making a good first impression. She returned to the lobby and nervously paced the tile floor. A painful course in Life 101 had taught her not to hope, but she wanted the job more than she dared to admit. The position paid better than most summer jobs and the buses ran regularly from the industrial park to a stop less than half a block from her condo. She knew a typing test would be required, but if she could make it past the initial interview, that didn't worry her.

Finally she was led to an office.

Ms. Whitehall, the personnel director, offered Jade the seat across from her desk. "Just give me a moment to read over the application."

Jade nodded and used the time to look around the rather cluttered office. Gray file cabinets held memo bins stacked high with papers. A pile of applications sat in the corner of the black steel desk, and Jade wondered how many people had applied for the few temporary openings. She compared her own navy blue dress to the stylish beige business suit of Ms. Whitehall and began to lose hope of getting the position.

Jade, who lived her life without most sounds, could still feel the silence in the room. Several times Ms. Whitehall raised her head to look at Jade with an awkward smile that she had come too recognize too well. Anyone could guess by her references that she was hearing impaired. Her high school, college, and even her teaching jobs were all at deaf institutes.

"Do you understand me?"

Jade nodded.

"Let me tell you a little bit about the job first." Ms. Whitehall went on to explain the duties. She was polite to the point of insulting as she gave the standard, rehearsed speech on company policy and a job description. "Do you have any questions?"

Jade shook her head. What was the point? Apparently, she was going to be dismissed without so much as a typing test. To be passed over because she was unqualified was acceptable, but not being given a chance to prove herself had her seething with rage and ready to pick a fight with a heavyweight boxer.

Ms. Whitehall stood up. "You should be hearing from us. . . . I'm sorry . . . I meant . . ."

Jade shrugged. If she were lucky she would be receiving a standard form letter in the mail in the next few days. Holding her head high, she exited the office and went quickly to the lobby. She reached for the door at the same time she felt a hand clamp down on her wrist. An angry outburst died on her lips and she looked up into the eyes of Luke Clayborne.

"Robert has been delayed a few minutes," he said, leading her away from the exit.

Numbly, Jade followed. She couldn't believe he had made a special trip to deliver that message. Particularly when their last meeting had been so unfriendly.

"Just sit for a moment." He gently guided her back into the seat in the lobby. Although he didn't sign, she had no problem understanding his words. Years of living with his sister must have taught him that he had to speak slowly while maintaining eye contact if he wanted half a chance of receiving a response. "Would you like coffee or tea?"

Jade declined with a shake of her head. She wanted to leave. Though no one questioned their return to the lobby, the situation must have appeared odd. Yet they weren't given a second glance. The few people who did pass apparently knew Luke well. Only when a woman stopped to get his signature did Jade realize he was more than a visitor. He was the boss!

She scrambled out of the chair at the same time Robert came bursting through the front door. "I'm sorry," he signed and spoke at the same time. "I had a small fender bender on my way in."

Jade's anger slipped away. Her petty embarrassment seemed juvenile compared with Robert's troubles. Especially since he had only come there to help her. Or had he? She knew he worked for his cousin. She gazed up at the two men who stared curiously at her.

"I have to leave. . . ." she signed.

"Your interview?" Robert reminded her.

Jade gave him a brief summary of her less-than-promising interview. She stopped short of adding that she would rather have had an accident herself than go through the process again.

Luke, who did little more than stare at her through the exchange, stepped sideways to block her path as she tried to leave. Although she was not considered short by any means, he towered a full head over her.

"What's going on?" he asked.

She signed an answer, knowing full well that he didn't understand one word.

"You know I don't sign." Her hands flew up in disgust and Luke quickly grabbed her wrist. "That sign I already know, thank you. Robert can tell me what happened."

His hand held hers in a firm yet surprisingly gentle grip. He smiled and she found herself drowning in the warm brown eyes that watched her. Her pulse rate accelerated but she refused to credit his touch with the phenomenon. She was experiencing a physical reaction to a stress-filled morning. Nothing more. So why had she allowed him to continue to hold her hand while he spoke to Robert?

Perhaps it was just as well she hadn't gotten the job. Working for Luke Clayborne could destroy her peace of mind.

Chapter Two

A gentle breeze floating across her back let Jade know that quitting time had arrived. Three weeks on the job and already she knew the routine. The speed at which the building cleared out on Fridays was a source of amusement and amazement.

After a rough first week, she had settled into her job nicely. Madeline, the data entry clerk who had trained her, seemed to think that yelling would help. Jade heard nothing, but everyone else did. Except for an odd question, Jade made sure she mastered the system quickly. Opening up mail orders and keypunching the information into the computer didn't require an exorbitant amount of skill.

Her coworkers were polite and tried to include her in their conversations, but Jade found little in common with them. She was paid to work, not socialize, and the fact that Luke had directly intervened on her behalf left her feeling she had to work harder to prove herself.

Once the office was empty, she straightened her desk and took a few minutes to file the completed work. She still had another fifteen minutes before the bus arrived. While leaning over her keyboard to log off her system, she noticed a shadow on the wall. The person remained motionless, watching her. The bitter memory of cruel jokes her brother had played on her set her other senses on alert. Only when she smelled the lingering scent of a familiar cologne could she relax and smile. Without a glance she wadded up a piece of paper and tossed it over her shoulder.

The shadow ducked and then walked over to her desk. "How did you know it was me?" Robert asked.

She stood and glanced around the office to be sure they were alone.

"Get real, Jade. It's Friday. Everyone's gone home already."

"Just checking," she said.

"Why do you still feel shy to speak in front of them? You have a beautiful voice."

"It's not that. I have nothing to say on the subject of Madonna, MTV, or the local bars."

Robert rose to the defense of their colleagues with a wry grin. "That's not all they talk about."

"True. They talk about what a hunk your cousin is, but that's another subject I'd prefer not to discuss."

He laughed and she imagined that he must have a deep, rich laugh. She had a fading memory of her own father's voice from her childhood and she automatically superimposed that voice on any man she was fond of.

"If you dislike him as much as you claim, why do you work for him?"

"It's not his warm and winning personality. He pays well and I need the money."

"If you gave him a chance you'd discover that Luke's not that bad."

"Not to look at. I guess I wouldn't strain my eyes when staring at him, but..." An odd expression crossed Robert's face and she automatically lowered her voice. "Am I speaking too loud?"

"No."

"Then what's wrong?"

He rolled his eyes and laughed again. The embarrassing suspicion that they were no longer alone was confirmed as she pivoted around slowly.

"You can talk," Luke said.

"Very good. Now we know why you're the president of this company," she blurted out before she could stop herself. "Sorry," she gestured, automatically reverting to signing as a defense mechanism.

"I only meant that I've never heard you speak so I assumed that like Kyle, you don't."

Robert shook his head. "Like Kyle, she chooses not to talk. At least not with you."

The slight grin dropped from Luke's face. "What has she got against me?"

Robert shrugged. "Fight it out with her. I have a date tonight and I wouldn't want her to leave without me."

"Robert . . . Robert . . . Ugh!" She stomped her foot. How could he leave her? Luke couldn't have missed her earlier comments about him. A cowardly retreat was in order. She grabbed her purse from the desk and waved good-bye.

He caught her wrist. "Oh, no you don't. We are having a discussion."

"You are. I'm catching a bus," she signed spitefully.

"You know I don't understand. At least *tell* me what I've done to cause this resentment."

"That *is* the problem," she snapped out. "I shouldn't have to tell you. After eighteen years of living with your sister, you should be fluent in Sign Language. It's unforgivable."

What did she see reflected in his brown eyes? Hurt, a sad sense of agreement? "I didn't live with her. She's lived at a residential school since she was four years old."

"That's no excuse."

"I know," he said simply. "I travel so often for work that I could never find the time to attend a class."

"I don't buy that either. Hire a private tutor to teach you at your convenience. It's not like you can't afford it."

Luke swallowed a chuckle. Few employees had the nerve to disagree with him, let alone tell him off. "You're right. So, when can you start?"

"I beg your pardon?" Her stunned question apparently didn't come from a lack of comprehension but rather shock.

"You need money and I need a tutor. It's a perfect arrangement."

"Perfect for whom?"

"For both of us," he said. "Come on, we can discuss this over dinner."

"I can't. I . . . uh . . . I have to catch a bus."

"I'll drive you home after we've ironed out the details."

"I don't want to teach you."

"But you do want me to be able to communicate with Kyle, right?" She paused, and he thought perhaps she didn't understand the question. He placed a finger under her chin and tipped her head back. "I said—"

"I know what you said." She removed his hand and stepped beyond his reach.

"So?"

"So, what? If I agree, I have to teach you. If I disagree then I'm condoning your silence with your sister, which you know, I don't."

He smiled. "Good."

"Don't get too sure of yourself. You haven't heard my price yet."

"I'll pay it regardless."

"No amount of money will restore your relationship with Kyle. Some things can't be bought."

Jade had the wrong impression about his motives.

For the past few years he felt as if his sister had been shutting him out. In his arrogance, he never realized that his failure to learn her language had left her feeling the same way. He couldn't begin to restore his relationship with her until he could make her understand him. And Jade Allenwood held the key that would allow him to unlock the door to Kyle's world.

"So, do we grab a bite while we work out the details?"

"No. When you've figured out some kind of schedule, let me know and I'll see if it conflicts with mine."

She had no trouble expressing her displeasure with him. Except for a slight hollow tone, her voice was nearly flawless and filled with emotion.

"You seem upset. Why?"

"I don't like being manipulated, Mr. Clayborne, which is exactly what you did. I'm not sure what your game is, but—"

He waved his hand to cut her off. "Back up. What makes you think this is a game?"

"It better not be."

"I'm very serious about learning to sign and I'm willing to devote as much of my free time toward that goal as I can."

Her wide eyes sparkled like two emeralds. "Well, I don't have a lot of free time to waste, so the minute I feel you aren't serious, our arrangement is over."

"Fair enough. When can we start?"

Jade checked her watch. So much for catching the 5:15 bus. "Shoot."

"What's wrong?" he asked.

"Forget it," she mumbled.

In the three weeks she had been working at Direct Mail she had done everything in her power to avoid him. Now she knew her instincts had been right. He had only been in her life for ten minutes and already he was fouling it up. She had an uneasy feeling that she would live to regret this.

Luke touched her arm. A warmth began where his fingers rested and spread through her. She raised her head and locked her gaze on him. Her body trembled. She couldn't concentrate on what he was saying even though she stared straight into his handsome face.

She shook her head violently to clear her mind. "I'm sorry. What did you say?"

His cocky half-grin was too much for her. Apparently he knew that her hearing deficiency wasn't responsible for her lack of comprehension. He, too, had noticed her response to his touch.

For goodness' sake, Jade, get a reality check. You've gone this route before. Men like Luke Clayborne didn't have the slightest understanding of her world.

"I was asking what your weekends are like?"

She exhaled an angry groan. "They're pretty much the same as any normal person's. I clean my house, visit friends, maybe take in a museum."

He cupped her chin between his thumb and forefinger, forcing her to look at him. "I never meant to imply that you weren't normal. I meant as far as the lessons go. Are you free on weekends?"

"Oh," she grumbled. Perhaps she was being overly defensive but with Luke, it came easy. "I suppose so."

"Is tomorrow good?"

Her eyes rounded in surprise. "Tomorrow? Give me time to arrange things."

"You want time to change your mind. That I won't give you."

She turned her head to free herself from his hold. "I'm a business teacher. You might be better off with someone who actually teaches Sign Language."

"I'll risk my money on you."

He was stubborn, she'd grant him that. Whether he was determined enough to follow through or just trying to ease his conscience remained to be seen. "All right. Then we'll begin tomorrow, Mr. Clayborne."

He caught her arm as she started to leave. "We're going to be spending a lot of time together. When are you going to stop calling me Mr. Clayborne and start calling me Luke?"

"When you can tell me what to call you in my language," she signed and answered at the same time. She might as well get him used to the process from the beginning.

To her surprise, he spelled out the letters of his

name with his fingers. ''Luke,'' he said when he finished.

''So, you do know some signing already.''

''Just the alphabet, but it's a start. Right?'' He arched one eyebrow hopefully, like a child looking for praise from a parent. Her heart fluttered and a smile tugged at the corner of her mouth. He could be captivating when he wanted to be.

And she was playing right into his manipulating hands again. The man wielded his charm like a soldier wielded his weapon. Only Luke's charm might be infinitely more dangerous.

She shook her head and muttered, ''I know the Greek alphabet. Doesn't mean I speak Greek.''

''You're not going to give me a break, are you?''

''No.'' She couldn't afford to. Theirs was a business relationship. In a one-on-one teaching situation, she needed to remain detached. Not that she had ever managed that feat with her students.

''All right.'' He paused, then added, ''For now. What time tomorrow and where?''

''After ten o'clock at my condo.'' In her home she would have the advantage of familiar surroundings, and she would need every advantage when it came to dealing with Luke. She jotted down the address on a piece of paper from the desk and handed it to him.

This time he didn't stop her as she turned to leave. She was far too aware of him. Apparently she hadn't learned from the mistakes in her past. She would do well to remember what life had been like with her own brother. Not to mention her brief yet painful broken engagement. As soon as she got home she was going to take a nostalgic stroll down memory lane. If that didn't cure her, she would try something more drastic before tomorrow.

Luke wrote the last check and closed the check-book. He raised his hand to the base of his neck and massaged the tight muscles. Despite the discomfort, he grinned. For the past three weeks he'd been trying to come up with a way to ask Jade about teaching him to sign. Things couldn't have worked out better if he'd planned them. Her acceptance had been less than en-thusiastic, but she had agreed.

He closed his eyes and called her image to mind. Having her in the office proved to be more of a dis-traction than he'd anticipated. She kept to herself, which might explain why he'd failed to notice that she could speak. But that was the only thing about Jade Allenwood that he'd failed to notice. He found himself thinking about her far too often. She was an employee and therefore off limits. At least until the end of the summer.

"You seem to be in a good mood, Lucas."

Luke glanced toward his mother, Vivian, as she en-tered the study. "I am." He put the checkbook in the top drawer and pushed away from the desk.

"Are you finished there?" she asked.

"Yes. I've taken care of everything."

"You always do, dear."

Luke wasn't sure, but he thought he noted a trace of sarcasm in his mother's voice. He had always taken care of her finances, even after he had moved out. She had never given him any indication that she wanted to change that arrangement.

"Where's Kyle?" he asked.

"In her room. She's tired."

Either his sister needed a vitamin injection or she was avoiding him again. Kyle always seemed to be tired when he came to the house. "Will she be down for dinner?"

"Are you staying?"

"Is one dependent on the other? Will she only come down to eat if I leave?"

Vivian shrugged and smiled sadly. "What do you want me to say?"

"Never mind." He rose and grabbed his jacket off the back of the chair. So much for his good mood.

As he passed his mother, she put a restraining hand on his arm. "Go talk to her."

"Why? She obviously doesn't want to see me."

"That's no reason to stop trying."

Actually, he thought it was a pretty good one. He wasn't a glutton for punishment. Despite the fact that his family believed him to be a computer incapable of human emotion, he could only take so much. "All right. I'll go see her before I leave."

He strode down the corridor to Kyle's room but hesitated outside the door. What could he say, assuming she made the effort to understand him? He heard a steady stream of tapping and figured she was working on her computer. Maybe he shouldn't disturb her.

Before he talked himself into leaving, he pushed the button on the wall to flash the lights in her room. The typing stopped and a set of footsteps shuffled across the carpet. Kyle's bright smile faded the moment she saw him.

Without a word, she turned and went back to her computer. Not an overwhelming response, but at least she hadn't slammed the door in his face.

She typed out a sentence, then paused as the computer-generated voice said, "What do you want?"

Since she refused to look at him, Luke had no choice but to type his answer. "I wanted to talk to you."

"Why?"

"Do I need a reason?" He hated communicating in this impersonal manner and for the first time realized that Kyle must feel the same.

"You usually do."

"That's not true." In his frustration, he made two typographical errors.

She snickered at his ineptitude. "Well, now you've seen me. That should hold you for another year."

"Kyle," he said. He placed his thumb under her chin and tilted her head back. "I'm sorry."

She gave no indication that she understood. Refusing to use a cold machine to make his point, he spelled the words out with his fingers.

For one long moment she could only stare. What did he see reflected in her eyes. Surprise? Hope? Whatever she had been feeling, he'd never know. Her expression changed to a mask of hostility and she turned her attention to the keyboard.

"If that's all, I'm rather busy," she typed. Her fingers drummed out her anger in a staccato rhythm. He couldn't force a confrontation. All she'd have to do is pull the plug on the computer and he'd be lost. He had to wait until he could explain himself in her language.

On the drive home he thought about the time and distance that had passed between them. Despite their differences, they apparently had more in common than their surnames. Both he and Kyle related better to the computer than to each other. He would find a way to communicate with her no matter how long it took.

First he had to work his way through the maze of distrust surrounding Jade Allenwood. Not an easy task, but one he was up for. He needed a challenge in his life. With his business running successfully and smoothly, he had plenty of free time; a luxury he hadn't known in the past fourteen years.

Chapter Three

Jade closed the front door and leaned back against the wall. The scent of musk and sandalwood surrounded her. Her condominium had seemed so much bigger before Luke had arrived. She glanced at her watch. If nothing else, the man was punctual, to the minute. She'd barely had time to finish cleaning and get set up. Any normal person would know that ten o'clock on a Saturday morning was an indecent hour to come calling no matter what the reason.

Unlike the rest of the world, he probably didn't need sleep. He could just plug his circuits into an outlet at night and recharge his batteries. She looked at Luke filling the easy chair in her living room and revised her image of him as a cold, calculating machine. Dressed in jeans and a fitted black pullover, he was pure male in a very attractive package.

Had she really thought that opening her home to him would give her some kind of advantage?

"We should get started." She crossed the room and knelt down in front of the coffee table. "Besides the alphabet, how much signing do you know?"

"Do I include the gestures you frequently share with me?"

Warmth flooded her cheeks. "Nasty gestures aside."

"None. I learned the alphabet from a book."

She shook her head. "Books aren't much help in this case. I pulled out some videotapes you can borrow. The one I'm about to put on explains the basics of signing better than I could. So I'll make us coffee while you watch it."

"You don't have to."

She stifled a yawn. "Yes I do. Cream and sugar?"

"Fine."

After pushing the play button, she went to the kitchen to make herself a dose of caffeine. While she waited for the coffee to brew, she leaned across the counter and gazed into the living room.

Luke had perched on the edge of the chair and stared at the screen. A few times he tried to imitate the gestures and even rewound the tape at one point to try again. His very nature was the antithesis of language. Where signing required animated gestures and facial expressions, Luke's rigid control made him seem like a robot.

"Loosen up," she called out.

He hit the pause button and turned toward her. "If I can't get hand positions right, how am I ever going to learn?"

"Did you think you were going to learn it all in one

hour? If you lived the language twenty-four hours a day it would still take months to become even semi-fluent.''

He lowered his head and grumbled something.

''I didn't catch that. You have to look at me if you want me to understand.''

He shrugged and met her gaze. ''Sorry. It's easy to forget with you.''

Absently, she twirled a strand of hair around her finger. ''Not for me.''

He opened his mouth to answer but she cut him off.

''Finish the tape and then I'll show you the hand positions.''

Luke did his best to concentrate on the rest of the video but his thoughts more often than not wandered to his hostess. Her bright, sunny condominium, with its nautical motif, felt as serene as a calm ocean. Much like Jade herself. At least on the surface. Had he detected the beginnings of a storm beneath her placid exterior?

He tried to imagine what her world was like, but he couldn't. As a teacher she must be good. According to his mother, she was a favorite among the students, particularly Kyle. In the office she was a dedicated worker whose output exceeded most of the others. She was driven, that much he could tell, but what motivated her? As a workaholic, she came close to rivaling him.

He didn't realize that the tape had ended until Jade

placed a tray on the coffee table and hit the stop button. He raised his shoulders in apology.

"It's a lot to absorb all at once," she said. "It's not like learning a foreign language. Every word in English doesn't have a translation. Each sign stands for a concept or idea, not an actual word."

"That makes it harder."

"Many of the signs look like the concept they're conveying so they're easy to remember." She sat cross-legged on the floor and passed him a steaming mug of aromatic brew. "Look at the bright side. You won't have to conjugate verbs." Her expressive smile lit a dark corner somewhere deep inside him. He must be a sucker for green-eyed optimists.

He took a sip of coffee and leaned back in the chair. "May I ask you something?"

"You can ask. I won't promise I'll answer."

"Why is your speech so clear compared to Kyle's?"

"Is it?"

"You know it is."

She raked a hand through her mane of curls. "I've been told. I wouldn't know anymore."

"Anymore?"

Apparently he had touched on a delicate subject. Her eyes narrowed and she chewed on her bottom lip. "I'm not deaf. I'm hearing impaired."

"What's the difference?"

"I lost most of my hearing in an accident when I was twelve but I can still hear to a certain degree."

"To what degree?"

"On the right side, I hear about forty percent of what you do if I wear my hearing aid. My speech was learned while I could hear, unlike your sister, who had to undergo years of speech therapy."

"What kind of accident?"

She exhaled a groan. "You're not paying me to learn my life history. Believe me, it's not all that exciting anyway." The defensive tinge to her voice wasn't lost on him.

"It's my money."

"Well, it's my time. Shall we continue?"

He grinned wryly. "By all means, teacher."

"Then pay attention and watch me."

He slid down to the floor to meet her at eye level. She took authoritative control of the lesson, treating him like a teenage student she considered a discipline problem. Gradually, her wariness subsided and she relaxed in his presence.

Several times he deliberately made mistakes so she would cover his hands with hers and show him the correct way to make the sign. As she took him through the different hand shapes and movements that made up each sign, she became downright animated. Although she may not have intended anything personal, her long slender fingers roaming freely over his hand and arm sent a jump start to the dead battery he called a heart. He drew on every ounce of willpower he possessed to squelch the impulses her touch incited in him.

"Now you try," she said, almost on cue.

He swallowed hard. Try what? Try running his hands over her?

Try concentrating on the lesson before she tosses you out the door. "I'm sorry. What did you say?"

She shook her head and laughed. "And I'm the one with the hearing problem?"

He had an entirely different kind of problem. He had never been drawn to any woman he worked with. Heck, he'd never been this drawn to any woman, period.

"Maybe we should take a break for a while," she said. "You're probably feeling a bit . . . overwhelmed . . ."

"You have no idea," he muttered.

"It's not unusual."

He cocked his eyebrow. "It's not? This happens often to you?"

"Well, not to me personally, but for me, it's different."

"Oh. How so?" He tried to suppress the smile twitching at the corners of his mouth. She was so serious.

"Well, I teach basic computers and business-related courses."

"What does that have to do with anything?"

"People don't often go out and work themselves into a lather about the merits of a hard drive over floppies."

He couldn't contain his laughter. "What are you talking about?"

"I'm talking about how overwhelming it can seem when you're first learning to sign. What are *you* talking about?"

"I was referring to this overwhelming attraction between us."

"Oh." Her eyes widened. "Oh," she said again.

A warm flush rushed to her cheeks. She scooted backward. The distance didn't lessen her awareness of him. Twenty-eight years old and she was blushing like a flustered adolescent who had a crush on a movie star.

"Unseasonably warm weather we're having, huh?" he said. He didn't even have the decency to look embarrassed.

This would not do at all. She was no better than the kids she taught. Luke was her student, nothing more. She didn't even like the man. He was pushy, manipulative, and too arrogant for her tastes. So why didn't she deny that she felt an attraction toward him? "Maybe we should call it a day."

"I can get my mind back on the lesson. Unless, of course, you can't . . ."

"I can," she shot back. His ego was incredible.

"Good. We can continue." Flecks of gold danced

in his eyes. Too late, she realized that she had been outmaneuvered again.

"I think I'll go back to using the videotapes for now."

His broad grin mocked her. "I was enjoying the hands-on instruction."

"Apparently more than I had intended," she grumbled as she pushed up to her feet. "Pop in tape number two."

She retreated to the kitchen to prevent further conversation. Her body ached with uncharacteristic yearning. *Get a grip. You'll never be more than an amusing pastime to him. Haven't you learned anything?*

Memories of her ex-fiancé cooled her as effectively as a bucket of ice water. She had met Steven when he was a young lawyer working for Legal Aid. She fell for the charismatic man who seemed genuinely committed to championing the causes of the underdog. But Steven was committed only to himself.

Once he worked his way into a prestigious Hartford law firm, he shed his ideals faster than his store-bought suits. Custom-made clothes, a flashy car, and an overpriced townhouse were part of the package he sold as himself. A deaf fiancée, no matter how well he dressed her up, didn't fit his new image.

Since then, Jade had avoided romantic entanglements. And she intended to keep on avoiding them. Particularly with Luke Clayborne, a man whose actions toward his sister proved he was no different than her ex-fiancé. As long as she kept that in mind, she would have no trouble keeping their relationship professional.

She opened the refrigerator and picked though the contents. Luke couldn't stay glued to the television indefinitely. She might as well use lunch as a way to give him some practical applications of signing. Once she made the sandwiches and laid out the table, she had run out of excuses to avoid him.

"Luke," she called out to him. "Lunch is ready."

He joined her in the kitchen. "I planned to take you out to lunch."

"You did?" she asked skeptically. "Then why did you wait until I finished making the sandwiches to tell me?"

"I didn't think you would go."

"Well, you're wrong." She signed and spoke slowly at the same time. "You're paying me to teach you, not feed you. So you're going to have to work for your food today. Anything you want, you have to ask for in sign."

"Anything?"

She ignored the seductive glint in his eye. "You can study the tapes for months, but you'll only learn by doing. If you were paying attention to that last video, you should have retained enough to make it through lunch."

"And if I forget a sign here or there I starve?"

"Then spell the word, since that's what you'll have to do when you talk to Kyle."

Throughout lunch Jade had to hold back a laugh at the way Luke struggled with the signs. Now she knew why women took to the language so much easier. Where she was naturally expressive even when she spoke, Luke rarely gestured with his hands. His body was as controlled as his mind.

He exhaled an immense sigh of relief when lunch was finished and he could revert to speech. Jade tried to curb the disappointment she felt. She hadn't expected him to be fluent after two hours of lessons but she had hoped he would begin to feel comfortable with the language. Maybe he would give up and she would be released from her agreement. Oddly, she didn't care for that option but she refused to contemplate why.

Luke stood at the sink and plunged his hands into the soapy water. When he had offered to take care of the dishes he never thought she would accept. Maybe he should have. Nothing about Jade was what he expected. She aroused feelings that he would be wise to suppress.

She worked for him, a point she drove home by asking him to fill out a time card for the hours of teaching. Right now, he needed her help. He couldn't afford to anger her. So, if he knew he should back away, why had he ignored her implied hint for him to leave?

Because she intrigued him.

Jade had a passion for her work that he would bet carried over into other areas of her life. He'd like to find out for himself. Angered by where his wandering thoughts were leading him, he adjusted the tap for cold water and splashed some onto his face. Curiosity was a dangerous emotion, and one he could ill afford—yet.

He glanced into the living room where Jade had settled into the corner of the sofa. She stretched her long, denim-clad legs out in front of her and rested her feet on the edge of the coffee table. He was a patient man. He could wait. With the last dish washed and left to dry in the drainer, he joined Jade.

"When is our next lesson, Teach?"

Her eyebrows arched in question. She was staring straight at him, so he knew she understood, but instead of answering, she tapped her finger to her ear. "Excuse me? I can't hear. What did you say?"

"Are you going to make me sign?"

She nodded.

"I feel like I'm speaking broken English," he said as he spelled out the words and combined it with one sign.

"There's no shame in speaking broken English, or Sign Language for that matter. The shame is in not trying because you're not perfect at it."

"Is there a message in that besides the obvious?"

"Yes, but I have a feeling it would be lost on you

right now.'' She came to her feet and collected the videotapes from the table. ''Practice, and I'll see you on Monday or Tuesday after work.''

''We could go to dinner first.''

''I don't think so. You're not ready for field trips yet.'' She put the tapes into a plastic bag and handed it to Luke.

''Are you trying to make me leave?'' he asked, and even managed to make the correct sign for *leave.*

A smile covered her entire face. ''I knew you'd be a quick study.''

''You didn't answer my question.''

''Yes, I did.''

Once he got to his car, he let out a hearty laugh. Jade didn't waste her time with subtlety. She said what she meant and she didn't bother to candy-coat her words. He liked that. He also liked that she was off-balance around him. No matter how much she wanted to deny it, there was an attraction between them. Enough to make him question his long-standing resolution to avoid relationships with employees.

Her position was temporary. She had clearly pointed out on her application that she planned to return to her teaching position in September. That put her in a different class than the women who might feel intimidated about the long-term prospects of their jobs if they dated the boss. He laughed again. He was rationalizing, and not very well, a character trait he often scorned in others.

He thought about the way she ushered him out of her house. All his rationalizations might be for nothing. Jade didn't appear anxious to explore the unexpected and highly charged electricity between them. On the contrary, she seemed to want to pull the plug.

Chapter Four

Jade coasted the last fifty yards of the sidewalk to her front door. The one-hour Rollerblade cruise around the sleepy Connecticut town had worked up a good sweat, but she hadn't cleared her thoughts of Luke Clayborne as she had hoped. So much for keeping a detached distance. She'd had her hands all over his, and worse, she had enjoyed herself.

The exercise hadn't helped to relieve her frustration. Maybe a pound of chocolate might. She flopped onto the bench on her porch and bent over to untie her skate. Beads of perspiration rolled down her face and she ran a hand across her forehead.

She saw the shadow at the same time she felt a hand clamp on her shoulder. A gasp stuck in her throat. Her heart seemed to stop, then began racing wildly.

Scream, she thought, but no sound came. A shiver crawled up her spine. Fear, acute and painful, brought a foul taste to her mouth.

The hand that held her suddenly relinquished its grip. She sprung from the bench and whirled around, a move difficult to control while still in her Rollerblades. Bracing herself against the wall, she raised a glare at her attacker.

For one eternal moment she could only stare. Then her panic was replaced with a violent anger for a man who should have known better.

"Anton, you're such a jerk," she snapped.

"Is that any way to greet your brother?"

As if sneaking up from behind on a sister he knew couldn't hear him was the epitome of a sensitive and loving brother. He rarely had the time or inclination to visit her, which only meant one thing. "How much do you need?"

"Right to the point, huh, Isabella?"

She winced. Somehow he always managed to make her given name seem like an insult. Perhaps that was why she preferred her nickname. "Would you be here otherwise?"

"You do go out of your way to make me feel welcomed after all."

She didn't need to hear to catch his sarcasm. As usual, he turned the situation around to make himself the wronged party. Chronologically, Anton was two years her senior, but he acted like an irresponsible teenager who couldn't seem to make his allowance last the week. She only saw him when his rent was due, or some other outstanding bill he didn't have the money for.

"You know I wouldn't ask if it wasn't an emergency," he said.

How many times had she heard that line from him? She ran an appraising gaze over his meticulous appearance. Designer sportswear from head to foot. Apparently, his wardrobe didn't suffer due to his sorry financial state. "You always say that."

"Do you think it's easy coming to you for money? How do you think it makes me feel, especially knowing that I was responsible for your losing your hearing?"

"It was an accident," she said for at least the thousandth time in their turbulent and bitter relationship.

He shoved his hands into his pocket and hunched his shoulders. "An accident that was my fault. Why don't you say it?"

"Because that's just what you want. An excuse for messing up your life. Well, I won't be that excuse. I'm sorry." She kicked off one skate, then the other.

"You're sorry, I'm sorry. Everybody's sorry, Isabella, but it doesn't change anything, does it?"

"Did you think it would?"

"How can you be so complacent all the time?"

Complacent? Was that how he saw her? Many times she had wanted to give into a fit of rage. When she couldn't remember her mother's voice or a favorite song. When she wondered about a bird's squawk or a baby's cry. But she didn't blame anyone.

"You gonna come in?" she asked.

"I can't stay. I'm meeting some friends. . . ."

That came as no surprise. Even on Christmas, he

had stayed only long enough to drop off a box of chocolates and pick up his present from her. "You have to come in so I can write the check."

He followed her in the front door. "I don't suppose you have cash? The banks aren't open today and . . . well, you know."

"How much?"

"A few hundred. I'll pay you back." He always promised but he never did.

Her ex-fiancé used to warn her that Anton would never stop taking as long as she kept giving. That might be true, but she never could say no to Anton.

She handed him the money. "You might try calling me between your visits so I know you're alive. I don't even know where you're living."

"You know I don't have a T.T.Y. phone." She saw no point in reminding Anton that he had hocked the Teletype machine she had bought him the year before.

"There are special operators available for translating."

"I don't want a translator to speak to my sister. I'd rather do it in person."

Probably because she was less likely to refuse his request for money when he was standing at her door.

With the cash tucked tightly in his jeans pocket, he left without so much as a thank you. *Heck of a day,* she thought as she slumped down in the chair. Both Anton and Luke! Perhaps she should introduce them. They had so much in common. Neither one had a clue about her world, but she couldn't seem to get them out of her life.

"Where have you been all day?" Robert greeted Luke as he walked in the front door of his apartment.

"What are you doing here?" He stepped into the large, dark study and dropped the nylon bag on the desk. After spending the morning at Jade's bright and airy condo, his own home felt like a tomb.

Robert glanced in the bag and grinned. "We were supposed to play racquetball today, but I see you got a little sidetracked."

Luke groaned. In his impatience to see Jade away from the office he had forgotten to cancel his plans with his cousin. He poured himself a glass of mineral water from the bar and dropped down into the cocoa brown leather sofa. "Sorry."

"So, you conned her into teaching you after all."

"There was no conning involved. I asked and she was more than happy to oblige."

Robert chuckled and settled in the chair across from Luke. "You're paying her, right?"

"Through the nose," Luke admitted reluctantly.

"No one said that easing your guilt would come cheap."

"I'm not . . . forget it. You wouldn't understand." For years Robert had been after him to learn Sign Language. Luke couldn't fault his cousin for thinking he might have an ulterior motive now.

"Actually, I do understand. She's something else," Robert said.

"Jade? She's a good teacher." If he had paid attention to anyone in his family instead of putting every ounce of his energy into the business, he might have learned that three years ago.

"She's a great teacher."

"But?"

Robert arched his eyebrow. "What do you mean?"

"You seem to want to qualify that statement."

"None needed. She's a great teacher. Extremely dedicated. I'd bet that if she ever starts to think you're serious about learning to sign, she'll stop taking money from you and do it for nothing."

Luke waved his hand in the direction of the videos he planned to memorize before Monday and exhaled a groan. "What does it take to convince her, or you for that matter, that I'm serious?"

"That's the point. We're not the ones you have to convince. Kyle is. And you'll never do that as long as you still believe you can keep your life in neat little compartments."

"I don't do that."

Robert started to say something, then shook his head. "Maybe I should keep my mouth shut. You've done a lot for me."

Luke had never kept a scorecard. The auto accident that had taken his father had also taken Robert's parents. Since then, Robert had lived with Vivian and

Kyle, more brother than cousin. "Make your point, Cuz."

"You have your work, your family, your social life, and occasionally a love life. But you keep them separate, never allowing the different areas to overlap. If you want to live that way, fine, but you can't keep that kind of control over the people in your life."

"You're wrong."

"Am I? I can't remember the name of the last woman you brought to the house to meet your family, can you? How often do you ask Kyle to meet you at the office so you can have lunch together? When was the last time you saw one of your employees outside of the office?"

"This morning," Luke said smugly.

"Yeah, because you wanted something from her. Just wait until you try to stick Jade in one of your tidy little compartments."

Luke grunted. Just because he occasionally gave his family helpful suggestions didn't mean he was controlling. What would have happened to the business and the family if he hadn't taken charge when his father had died? His mother had been in no emotional position to assume the responsibility. In fact, she had begged him to take care of things. At nineteen, he'd had all the obligations of a father of three and none of the fun getting there.

Work, family, social life, and relationships. The four compartments of his life. Did he really keep them separate as Robert claimed? If so, where did Jade fit? She worked for him. She was connected to his family through Kyle and Robert. He wouldn't mind seeing her socially. A relationship? That was a rhetorical question since he couldn't stop thinking about her.

"If you're not up for racquetball, I'll be off," Robert said, breaking into his thoughts.

"What do you mean, not up for it?"

"Well, I can understand if you're feeling the strains of your age. Now that you're over thirty, the old bones aren't what they used to be. . . ." Robert's smirk mocked him.

Luke sprung from the chair. His cousin needed to be taught a lesson, and he needed some physical exertion to relieve his pent-up frustration. "Put your money where your mouth is."

Jade pressed a hand to her growling stomach. She had forgotten to set her alarm and she'd had to run out the door without breakfast this morning. She glanced at her watch. Time to keypunch one more batch of orders before her lunch break.

Luke had passed through the office on several occasions, but other than a surprising sign of "good morning" when she had first arrived, he had not given her a second look. She might as well have been one of the potted plants. So much for the spark of electricity she had thought existed between them. This wouldn't be the first time she had read a man wrong.

After spending a restless night worrying about how she would face him today, she should be relieved. Instead, she was irrationally insulted. He should feel awkward and confused, like her.

Getting her mind back on her work, she quickly entered the last group of orders. As she stapled the stack together, she felt a soft rush of air drift over her neck. She turned and raised her head.

"You look awful," she signed.

Robert's weak smile faded. "Thanks." Exhaustion etched his handsome features. He rested his arm, which was wrapped in an Ace bandage, on top of the partition that divided the office cubicles. "Forgive me if I don't sign today."

"What happened?"

"Did you ever hear of sudden-death racquetball?"

Jade shook her head. "But I can figure it out. Little boys and their silly, competitive games. Well, I hope you learned something."

"Yeah, I learned not to tell Luke he's getting old. The second you tell him anything, he sets out to prove you wrong."

"Luke?" The same man who strode around the office today as if he'd done nothing more strenuous than push a remote control button all weekend?

"I don't know what happened between you guys on Saturday but he sure took it out on me."

Her jaw dropped. "Nothing happened."

"Ah." Robert nodded as if he'd received a revelation from the heavens. ''Then that explains his frustration.''

She smacked his arm. He winced. ''Serves you right. You're not even close on that one.''

''Then why are you blushing?''

She waved a hand in front of her face. ''I'm feeling faint with hunger, that's all.''

He cocked a disbelieving eyebrow at her but thankfully dropped the subject. ''Kyle will be here any minute. Care to join us for lunch?''

''Sounds good.'' Jade logged off her computer and collected her purse from the desk drawer. She followed Robert to the lobby where they met up with Kyle as she was walking in.

While Kyle had always been a bit of a rebel, her clothing today was more outlandish than normal and appropriate only for a bikers' convention. The black leather miniskirt and studded vest covered enough to keep her from being arrested but little else. Style aside, Jade couldn't imagine that the outfit was very comfortable.

Apparently Kyle wanted to get someone's attention. Judging by the stunned gape on Luke's face as he entered the lobby, she had succeeded.

''Where do you think you're going dressed like that?'' Luke asked, with what appeared to be great anger.

Although Kyle didn't acknowledge her brother's words, her malicious smile said she understood.

Robert stepped between them, halting Luke with a firm hand. Jade couldn't make out Robert's words from behind but he must have been convincing because Luke took a step back and made no further comment on Kyle's outfit.

Luke locked his gaze on Jade. "Where are you going?"

"Lunch," she signed.

"Care to join us?" Robert added.

Luke glanced toward Kyle. Her displeasure was evident in her tense stance. "I guess not."

Kyle grinned. Robert appeared almost relieved.

Despite the fact that Kyle's anger was justified, Jade couldn't help but feel sorry for Luke. She had always sympathized with the kid no one picked for the baseball team, or the one who sat alone at the lunch table.

What next? Bring them on the "Oprah" show to see if they could work out their problems? Why not bring her own family along? Topic: "Brothers Who Refuse to Learn Sign Language and the Deaf Sisters Who Resent Them."

She had to stop interfering in everyone's life as if it were her God-given right. This was between Kyle and Luke, and none of her business.

"Maybe we could bring something back for you," she said to end the uncomfortable silence.

"No thanks," Luke said. "I'll see you later. Enjoy your lunch." He turned and strode away.

Like she would have half a chance of enjoying her lunch now.

At the restaurant Jade picked at her chef salad. Although she had been ravenous earlier, her appetite seemed to have vanished. She might have understood if Kyle had shown the slightest bit of sorrow, or at the very least, mixed emotions. Instead the young woman was exuberant, visibly pleased by the way she had embarrassed and hurt her brother. Since the end of school, her anger had taken on a cruel, vindictive edge.

A hollow ache filled Jade. Was this her idea of staying out of other people's business?

Robert tapped her arm to get her attention. ''What's wrong?''

She shrugged. ''I guess I'm not as hungry as I thought. My stomach is upset.''

''Luke has that effect on people,'' Kyle signed.

Jade shot Kyle an annoyed glare. ''What are you doing?''

''To Luke?'' she asked.

''No. To yourself.''

Kyle settled down through the remainder of the meal and even looked properly chastised. Despite the change of attitude, Jade didn't kid herself. The war between the Claybornes was far from over.

She shook her head. Hadn't she known this would happen once Kyle returned home? She had warned Luke that he couldn't fix his relationship with his sister overnight. Why did she feel so lousy about being proven right?

Chapter Five

Luke extracted the keys from his pocket and strode across the parking lot. Kyle's spectacle at the office had topped off a rotten morning. Robert's assurance that his sister was only trying to get his attention didn't ease Luke's mind. How much further would she go the next time she felt like making a point?

He was almost at his car before he noticed Jade leaning against the sleek black sedan. Her cream-colored blouse had been pulled free from the waistband of a calf-length skirt. Dark brown ringlets framed her face. She pushed a handful of hair behind her ear and smiled sadly.

"Here to say I told you so?" he asked.

Her eyes narrowed in confusion. "About what?"

"Kyle."

"Would I be telling you something you didn't already know?"

"No."

"Then I see no point in rubbing it in."

No, that wasn't her style, Luke decided. "Did you enjoy lunch?"

"Not really."

Relief mingled with guilt. Relief that she wouldn't enjoy herself at his expense. Guilt that her lunch had been ruined because of his family problems. "Perhaps you'll let me make that up to you by taking you to dinner."

"No. But I will accept a ride home. We can stop off at the market and pick up something to eat. While I cook, you can try to impress me."

"And just how would one go about impressing a lovely and talented woman such as yourself?"

A soft giggle bubbled forth. "Not with sappy lines like that. Try impressing me with how much you learned in the past couple of days."

"You're all business."

"This is a business arrangement."

"So you keep reminding me." He opened the car door for her. "Or are you reminding yourself?"

She expelled a deep sigh and slipped into the passenger seat. During the ride to the market, then home, she avoided all conversation. If he turned his head to speak with her she became visibly nervous and his limited ability to sign was hampered by driving.

When they arrived at the condo, she rushed into her bedroom to change. She returned wearing a red-and-gold short set with a New England Patriots logo emblazoned on the front.

"A football fan?" he asked.

She stepped around the butcher-block counter that

separated the kitchen from the living room and began emptying the bags from the market. "It's a bit tame for my liking. I prefer hockey."

He grinned. "I bet you do."

"Enough slacking off. Use your hands. What you don't know, spell."

"I'll have you know, I memorized every one of those tapes."

"Then why are your hands still in your pockets? You can't sign like that."

Luke draped his suit jacket over a chair and began a verbatim demonstration of the videos she had loaned him. Jade divided her attention between cooking and watching him. While the signs themselves were nearly flawless, he lacked any facial expression to show surprise or question.

"So, what do you think?" he asked.

She cut a tomato in quarters and added the pieces to a salad. "Learn to speak while signing. It's easier to remember and helps the person you're addressing when you can't remember a particular sign."

"I feel self-conscious enough making the signs."

"Get over it." She pushed the salad bowl to one side. "How do you like your steak?"

"Rare," he said as he came around the counter to join her.

"Spell it." He stood close enough for her to feel the vibrations of his deep voice as he spelled out the word. "That's better. And don't make a face at me.

You might know the letters but you don't do them fast enough.''

''What does it take to please you?''

''Perfection.''

A long spiral of hair fell free from her loose ponytail. Luke pushed the curl behind her ear, grazing his knuckles over her cheek. Her eyes widened and a breath caught in her throat.

He smiled. Why did he have to smile?

Her eyes were drawn to the upturned curve of his full bottom lip. She raised her gaze higher to his long autocratic nose and finally settled on his eyes. Those eyes, as dark as chocolate, with a sinfully rich desire reflected in their depths.

Please, don't let me be gaping like a star-struck idiot.

What was it about Luke's touch that affected her so swiftly and so profoundly? And what was she going to do about it?

He spoke but she couldn't catch the words. ''I'm sorry. Could you repeat that?''

He ran his fingers through her hair and gazed into her eyes. ''Don't apologize. I said it's amazing.''

''What is?'' Her words tumbled out in a breathless whisper. *Back away,* she told herself, but her feet refused to cooperate. She was mesmerized by him.

''It's amazing the way your eyes match your name.''

She blinked. ''Jade isn't my real name. It's a nick-name.''

''What is your name?''

Jade hesitated. She had come to associate her name with another person, another life. A life that belonged to a twelve-year-old musical prodigy whose world revolved around Bach and the Beatles.

Salty tears welled in her eyes. How odd, that a simple question like ''what is your name?'' could provoke such powerful memories. ''Isabella.''

''It's a beautiful name.'' He cupped his hand along the side of her face. ''But Jade suits you better.''

For reasons she couldn't begin to understand, his declaration warmed her. ''Are you going to kiss me?''

His laughter caressed her neck. ''The thought had crossed my mind. Would you rather I didn't?''

''You might as well get it out of your system. Otherwise you'll just be distracted all evening and we won't get anything done.''

''I'll be distracted?'' His eyebrows arched in disbelief. ''You, on the other hand, don't care either way?''

''Maybe I'm a little curious. But only a little.''

His hands slid over her shoulders and down to her waist. He lifted her up to the edge of the counter.

''Is this what you're curious about?'' His mouth brushed lightly over her. Warm breath mingled.

She closed her eyes. A host of new sensations sent her reeling. Luke pushed the hair off her shoulder and peppered her face and neck with feather-light kisses. She inhaled his masculine aroma.

He lifted his head and met her gaze. An invisible cord seemed to be pulling her closer, as if her mind no longer had a will of its own.

She wasn't sure what she'd hoped to accomplish by this fool-hearted exercise, but falling into his arms definitely wasn't in the plan. With her last ounce of willpower, she pushed him back.

A rumble of protest vibrated in Luke's chest. His eyes widened and a boyish expression of confusion spread across his face. She wriggled out of his arms and slid off the counter to the floor, praying her legs would hold her.

"So, have you gotten it out of your system?" she asked, doing her best to sound unimpressed. Apparently, she hadn't pulled it off.

Luke burst out laughing. "Until the next time."

"There won't be a next time."

He placed his thumb under her chin and tipped her head back. "Do you intend to deny what just happened here?"

"No. I intend to ignore it. You'd be wise to do the same."

"Why?"

"I'm not looking for some quick, meaningless affair."

His face clouded over in a wounded scowl. "What makes you think I am?"

"You wouldn't fit in my world on a long-term basis."

"Maybe not. But you'd fit in mine."

"That's a very one-sided relationship. One where I do all the compromising."

He expelled an exasperated groan. "I didn't mean it like that."

"I know." She shrugged and stepped beyond his reach. "But trust me, that's how it would end up."

"Jade . . ."

She turned her head away, effectively ending the conversation. "I'd better start those steaks." She kept her back to Luke, hoping to hide the aching frustration she felt.

She had to get him out of her system. If anything, he was more in her system now than before he had kissed her. Her lips still burned from the memory. That's what she got for playing with fire.

Jade opened the oven and put the steaks under the broiler. Luke leaned against the counter. With her back to him, she forebade him from answering her claim.

Normally, he would cut his losses. What was it about her that made him stubborn? He didn't usually require a brick to the head before he gave up on a woman. Jade might not want to pursue the attraction between them, but he sure did.

He touched her arm to get her attention. "Can we talk about this?"

"There's nothing to talk about." She reached into the cabinet above her head and removed some plates. "Set the table, please."

The aroma of grilling meat permeated the air. No sense arguing on an empty stomach. He took the dishes from her outstretched hands.

"My pleasure. Anything else I can do for you?" He arched his eyebrows seductively.

"Sure. Clean my bathroom."

He ignored her sarcasm. Instead he grinned. "It's too early in our relationship for something that personal. Maybe when I know you better."

"You always have to have the last word," she grumbled.

"You don't have to listen."

"I don't."

He winced. "Jade, I'm sorry. . . ."

"For goodness' sake, don't start apologizing every time you make a reference to hearing. I picked the fight. I deserved it."

He nodded and said nothing.

"No comment?" she asked.

"And have you accuse me of getting in the last word?"

She laughed.

"I give up." Luke took the plates to the table, shaking his head. Winning over Jade was going to be a bigger challenge than learning to sign.

He recalled the quiet certainty in her earlier words.

"That's a very one-sided relationship. One where I do all the compromising." Obviously, she had spoken from experience.

He finished laying out the flatware. In his peripheral vision he noticed her watching him. She wasn't indifferent. So, why did she continue to fight him? He thought back to their conversation. In the entire time he hadn't made one attempt to sign with her despite the fact that she always signed if her hands were free.

Jade shut the door and leaned back against the wall. What had happened? Once she had put the dinner on the table, Luke had seemed to undergo a radical personality change. Instead of a predator, he had become the model student.

Although he watched her continuously, the hunger she had witnessed earlier had vanished. Instead, his interest took on a different kind of intensity. He asked questions, requested to learn specific signs, and generally did exactly what any teacher would ask of her student, and then some.

He learned quickly, but she had figured he would. With a computer for a mind, Luke rarely had to be told anything twice. She should be pleased. This is what she wanted, after all.

Why didn't she trust him? The man was up to something. Once again, she got the feeling that he was manipulating her, but to what end? With looks like his, she didn't imagine he was hurting for female company.

Whatever plans he had for her would have to wait. On his way out the door he had informed her that he would be away for the next few days on a business trip. At least she wouldn't have to face him tomorrow and try to pretend their kiss had never happened. She could save that awkward moment for sometime in the future.

Luke stepped from the car and drew in a breath of fresh country air. Four days in the smog and congestion of Hong Kong had been four days too many. He'd had trouble getting into the spirit of Christmas purchasing in June, but that was the nature of his mail-order business. Although the trip had been a success, he was glad to be back in Connecticut.

He checked his watch. Only three hours later than he had anticipated. With the delays and traffic from the airport, he arrived just in time for dinner at his mother's house. He didn't call first because he knew Kyle would make other plans if he had.

His body ached with jet lag. Maybe he should have gone home and slept for a few hours. Postponing the visit wouldn't change the outcome. He flexed the tightness from his muscles and walked though the front door. The thought of another confrontation with Kyle left him with an uneasy feeling of guilt. Was it too late to reach his sister?

Footsteps echoed through the corridor. Loosening the tie at his throat, he proceeded into the dining room. Vivian and Kyle glanced up.

"Hello," he signed.

Vivian's jaw sagged and Kyle dropped her fork.

"Lucas," Vivian muttered. "Why didn't you tell me you were coming? I would have held dinner."

"I only now . . ." He paused to find a sign close enough to his meaning. "Returned," he finally spelled.

"Who is this man?" Kyle signed to her mother.

Luke felt a sense of pride that he was understood. "How are you?"

"Confused," she signed.

His fluency ended there. Kyle began a rapid succession of gestures that he couldn't follow. He glanced toward his mother for help.

Vivian wrinkled her nose and shook her head. Kyle insisted that her mother translate. "She said, and I quote, 'my brother is too stuck-up to sign. You must be an alien who has taken over his mind.' And, as far as she's concerned, you can keep his mind."

He chuckled and signed, "Thank you."

"For what?" Kyle asked with her hands.

"The compliment," he spelled.

Kyle let out a puff of air and returned to her dinner. He noted a hint of a smile that she tried hard to suppress. Apparently he had made some headway. The very fact that she answered him was an improvement.

"Let me get a plate for you," Vivian said.

He waved his hand to decline. "I can't stay. I just stopped in to see if you need anything."

"No. We're fine."

"Okay." He nodded and turned to leave.

"Lucas?" At his mother's call he rotated back. "I guess they were right about Miss Allenwood."

"What do you mean?"

Vivian smiled knowingly. "Dean Stanton said she could reach even the most hopeless cases."

"You think I'm hopeless?" he asked.

Kyle's laughter said it all. Apparently his sister lip-read much better than she let on.

So, his family found him unredeemable. As he returned to his car, he wondered if Jade felt the same way about him. Did she see him as nothing more than her student, or had he invaded her thoughts as often in the past few days as she had invaded his? There was one way to find out. He could pay the teacher a visit.

Chapter Six

Jade put the finishing touches on her makeup with ten minutes to spare. She glanced down at her outfit. Dean Stanton would have a heart attack if he saw her dressed in this grunge look. She had made a bet with a few of her graduating seniors involving final exams. As a result she had to accompany them to the Rolling Stones concert. Aside from the fact that the Stones were popular in her parents' generation as well as hers, a concert wasn't a common outing for hearing-impaired students.

Regardless, she had lost the bet and she had to make the trek into Hartford with six of her most industrious students. She reached inside her jewelry box for her hearing aid. If Mick Jagger had the nerve to strut his stuff across a stage at fifty, she could listen to the man sing. The normal volume of a rock concert would be audible to her.

The light flashed in the bedroom, letting her know that someone was at the door. She tossed a baseball cap over her unruly mass of curls and grabbed her purse. The light flashed again.

"Oh, hold your horses," she grumbled as she pulled the door open.

She gazed up into Luke's eyes and her breath caught in her throat. A tingling sensation ran along her spine. She moistened her dry lips and tried to regain her composure. The mere sight of a man should not render her a speechless idiot.

He looked over her appearance with a wry grin. "You shouldn't have dressed up for me."

"What are you doing here?"

"May I come in?" Absently she nodded and allowed him to enter. He strode into the living room and plopped in the reclining chair as if he had every right.

"What do you want?" she asked.

"I told you I'd be back at the end of the week. I thought we could get a lesson in."

The initial excitement she had felt at seeing him faded rapidly. "Oh. And naturally, you assumed I would just be sitting home waiting for you to grace me with your presence."

"I'm sorry," he said, but he didn't appear to be sorry. "Do you have plans?"

"Yes, as a matter of fact I do. You should have called. Or maybe you don't know how to use the T.T.Y. phone."

He cocked his eyebrow at her jibe. "Of course I do."

"Then next time call first and save yourself the trip."

"Why are you so upset?" Luke remained completely calm, which only served to make her more angry.

"I'm upset because you think you can just show up whenever you want."

"I haven't even been home yet. I came straight here because I thought that this was more important than changing my clothes or picking up my messages. I'm sorry."

She let out a muffled grunt. "Don't make yourself out as some kind of saint and me the unreasonable shrew. You came here because you felt like it and you didn't care about my plans."

"Did anyone ever tell you that your eyes turn emerald green when you're angry?"

"Did anyone ever tell you that's the oldest line in the book?" she snapped back.

He shrugged and broke out in a broad smile. "What can I say? I don't do my best when I'm suffering from jet lag."

"Then go home."

"I need your help," he signed.

Was the word SUCKER indelibly etched into her forehead? All he had to do was bat those big brown eyes of his and she felt like a louse for trying to get rid of him.

"I really do have plans. I can give you a more advanced tape to study if you want."

"I'll take whatever help you can spare." His expression reflected just enough gratitude to appear sincere.

"You're good," she muttered. She crossed the room and pulled a couple of videotapes from the collection on the top shelf. "Tomorrow, if you're free, we can see how much improvement you've made."

"Thank you," he signed.

The lights in the living room flashed. "That's my ride."

He sprung from the chair and caught her hand as she reached for the door handle. She turned back, the motion causing her to stumble into his rock-solid body. Before she could stop him, Luke brushed a kiss over her mouth.

She took an unsteady step back. "I have to go."

"Have a good time." He opened the door and signed "hello" to the young man on the front landing.

Numbly, she waved to Luke and followed her student to the car. She was half a mile away before she realized that Luke had stayed in her condo rather than walking out with her.

Luke watched from the window until the car disappeared down the street. At least she was with a large group. Dressed as she was, in torn jeans and a floppy flannel shirt, he doubted she was looking to meet a man.

He walked around her condo without remorse. She

had left him alone there. What did she expect? Next time she would stay home and keep him in line.

Magazines covered the top of the coffee table. He glanced through the pile of medical journals and periodicals. She had dog-eared specific pages in each issue. He began to read through the articles, all of which dealt with a new surgical procedure to correct auditory nerve damage.

An odd feeling of remorse washed over him. Apparently she was collecting the information for a reason. A reason that was none of his business unless she chose to tell him. He restacked the magazines and popped the first tape in the VCR.

As Jade walked up the sidewalk, she noticed the black luxury sedan parked on the side street. She checked her watch. Why was he still at her condo at midnight? Bad enough she had spent most of the evening thinking about him. The band seemed to sing ''I Can't Get No Satisfaction'' just for her.

She unlocked the front door and stepped inside. A television screen of white snow greeted her. She ejected the videotape and hit the off button. At the other end of the room, Luke was sprawled out in the recliner. He must have had a serious case of jet lag.

Her instincts told her to wake him and send him home. She gazed at his sleeping form and her annoyance deserted her. She couldn't kick him out now. Tomorrow they would have to get a few rules straight about their arrangement.

She took a quilt from the closet and covered Luke. He stirred but remained sleeping. Her stomach fluttered. His face, relaxed and peaceful, was the most handsome she'd ever seen. She didn't understand his apparent interest in her, but when she saw him like this she wondered why she kept fighting him and herself. The urge to run her fingers through his hair nearly overcame her.

Only four hours ago she had been furious that he had shown up without calling. Now, she was imagining things about the man she had no business thinking.

You need sleep. Exhaustion is warping your mind.

She flipped off the light, plunging the room into darkness. Out of sight was definitely not out of mind. She padded across the carpet and made her way to the bedroom. After a good night's sleep she would be back to her wary, distrustful self—she hoped.

An annoying drone woke Luke from a sound sleep. He peered out through heavy eyelids at the flash of a shadow dancing by. Jade was up early.

''Rise and shine, Mr. Clayborne.'' Jade ran the vacuum past the chair several times before turning it off.

''I'm up,'' he grumbled, then realized she wouldn't hear. He pushed the blanket off and came to his feet. ''Good morning.''

She answered his sign with a glare. "I figured you'd be long gone by now."

"Without thanking my hostess for her kind hospitality? That would be rude."

"I wouldn't want you to be rude," she muttered sarcastically.

He bit back a smile. "Did you wake up in a bad mood? That will happen when you're out partying until midnight."

"How do you know what time I came home?"

"Lucky guess?" He raised his shoulders casually.

Her eyes widened and a rosy blush stained her cheeks. "You lying little rot. You were awake last night when I returned."

"I never said I wasn't and you never asked." He had fully expected her to call his bluff about being asleep and tell him to leave. Instead she had covered him with a blanket before going to bed herself.

She tugged at the frayed hem of her cutoffs. Her anger seemed to dissipate and she let out a small laugh. "Are you this devious with everyone, or have I been singled out for special treatment?"

He grazed his knuckle across her cheek. "I'm not devious, merely persistent."

"And what are you after?"

Her question threw him. "Excuse me?"

"What did you expect would happen? I mean, did you really want to stay here so that you could watch me clean my house first thing in the morning?"

"No."

"Then why?"

"Does there have to be a reason?"

"With you? I would guess so."

On that count, she was right. He never did anything without a reason, but he'd be darned if he could figure out why he had wanted to stay last night. "Do you have any plans for today?"

She gave a slight bow to her vacuum. "I plan to take a spin around the house with Hoover here, then I have some other chores to catch up on."

"In other words, nothing important." Her nostrils flared in anger. He threw his hands up in guilty surrender. "Only kidding. Could I possibly persuade you to spend the day with me instead?"

"Why would I want to irritate myself like that?" She smiled. "Only kidding."

He rubbed his hand over the stubble on his chin. "Is that a yes?"

"Only if you promise to sign today."

"I promise to use my hands today."

Her laughter echoed off the walls. "Nice try, but I'm not that naive."

"You're a tough teacher."

"And you're an incorrigible student," she countered smoothly. The humorous banter was a welcome relief from her suspicious jibes.

"Is that all we are? Teacher and student?"

Her expression became serious. "I work for you.

That's reason enough to keep our relationship strictly business. So allow me to delude myself into thinking your interest in me is purely academic.''

"Do you often lie to yourself?''

"Only when it comes to you.'' She turned and pushed her vacuum across the room to a small closet. "Just let me get changed and we can go.''

"So, this is where you live.'' Jade walked around the large, dark living room. The smell of lemon-polished wood hung in the air. Rich mahogany paired with heavy upholstered furnishings gave the place an oppressive feeling. Luke's apartment complex was less than twenty minutes from where she lived, but she felt as if she had arrived in another country.

"What do you think?''

"It's . . . big . . . and masculine.''

The corner of his mouth twitched. "Interesting choice of words.''

"No more interesting than your color scheme. I never realized there were so many shades of brown. Does that trend carry through the entire place?'' His apartment had at least twice the square footage of hers, yet the massive wood furniture made her claustrophobic.

"I'm afraid it does. Perhaps you can make a suggestion on how to brighten the room.''

"Easy. Five gallons of white paint and lose those ugly drapes.'' Jade regretted the words the second they were out. What right did she have to criticize? His girlfriend might have chosen the decor with his approval. "Of course that's just my opinion. I don't have to live here."

"No. You're right. It is a tomb in here. I never really noticed before. I'm going to have a quick shower. Make yourself at home."

At home in a tomb? Was he serious?

She left the darkness of the living room for the brighter study. Although the room held onto the solid wood motif, two large windows allowed light in. The eastern sun cast a glare on a baby grand piano at the far end of the room.

The instrument immediately drew her attention. It had been years since she had played. She ran her hand across the lustrous surface and lingered over the keys. At the touch of her fingers, a chord vibrated.

Did Luke play? Was the piano in tune?

She glanced at the sheet music on the stand. Chopin had always been one of her favorites. She played a few notes. Like riding a bicycle, she could still remember how. She could even remember how the piece had sounded when played by her teacher.

The memories took her back to a place she didn't want to go. Some pain even time couldn't diminish. In the last few years, with the technology in hearing aids improving, her auditory capacity had risen, yet she had never tried to play the piano again. When she had lost the ability to hear the music, the desire had died inside her. At least she thought it had.

She had refused to play because she might not be perfect. The scenario sounded all too familiar. How could she judge Luke for being afraid to learn signing when she was a coward herself?

Her hearing aid was still in her purse where she had put it last night after the concert. Fate or coincidence? Fate, she decided, as she put the device on her ear.

Luke heard the soft strains of Chopin as he dressed. Why would Jade put on the stereo? After a few more seconds, he realized that the music was not coming from the CD player but the piano. Had someone arrived while he was in the shower? He tossed a T-shirt over his head and proceeded barefoot to the study.

Pausing in the doorway, he listened while Jade finished the piece. She had a remarkable talent. After four years of forcing him to take lessons during his childhood, his parents had finally come to the realization that he was hopeless. He only ended up with the piano because his mother had wanted it out of the house after Kyle had been diagnosed as profoundly deaf.

Jade hit a wrong note and brought her hands down on the keys in anger. So there was a temper that drove her passion for music as well as her life. The more he discovered about her, the more complicated she became.

"Don't stop," he called out without thinking.

She jumped and swiveled on the bench. Her wide-eyed gaze met his. He felt a twinge of guilt for scaring her, but he was more surprised by the fact that she reacted at all.

"You heard me?" he asked.

She exhaled slowly. "Sort of. I knew you were speaking."

He sat down next to her. "You play very well."

"Do I?" She folded her hands primly in her lap.

"Odd question, since you heard enough to know you made a mistake."

"I didn't hear it as much as I felt it. Besides, it's been years since I played. I'm really out of practice."

"How many years?"

She tensed and inched away from him. "What difference does that make?"

"I'm curious."

"Why?"

He shrugged. "Because I'm interested in you."

Her nose crinkled in distaste. "Maybe you can take something to help you get over it."

Luke edged in closer. His thigh brushed against hers and she trembled. Her body wasn't sending the same signals as her words. "It's like having a cold. There's no cure. It just has to work itself out of your system."

"And knowing about my past will aid in your rapid recovery?"

"You're clever with words, Jade, but you're avoiding the real issue."

"Which is?"

"Us."

She shook her head. "You're not ready for 'us.' You don't have any idea what it entails yet."

"That's what I'm trying to discover."

"No you're not. To discover takes time. You want a quick answer."

He was used to quick results, the bottom line in business. And with most of his personal relationships, he realized. Taking the slow route would be a novel approach for him, but perhaps his interest might not wane as quickly as it had with past relationships.

"You may be right, Green Eyes, but I'm never going to discover if you shut me out completely."

"I don't—" She stopped and lowered her head.

A long silence followed. Apparently, her piano playing was a painful subject. If he could get her to talk about that, the rest would come easy. He draped his arm across her shoulders and gave her a comforting squeeze.

"Sixteen years," she said.

"What?"

"The accident that took my hearing also destroyed my piano playing. When I was released from the hospital, necessity forced me to trade my piano keys for computer keys and get on with my life. I never played again."

Her words took more out of her than she had expected, yet the revelation left her feeling lighter, as if a weight had been lifted. Or was it playing the piano again that had brought about this sense of freedom?

"Why don't you play anymore?"

"I would have thought that was obvious."

He furrowed his brows in confusion. "But you heard me talking to you."

Jade pushed back the hair from the side of her face to reveal the hearing aid. "Only since they perfected this baby. If the sounds are loud enough, I can hear."

"So why don't you wear it more often?"

Bitterness tinged her laughter. "People see this and they start talking to me like I'm three years old. I'd rather lip-read than deal with ignorance. I only use the hearing aid when I go to clubs or concerts."

"I'm sorry," he said as if he were personally responsible. Ironically, Luke was one of the few people she knew outside of the school who didn't talk down to her.

"Why?"

"I don't know."

"If you're gonna be sorry, at least have a reason."

He raised his gaze skyward then back to her. Warm breath rushed over her neck at his exhale of exasperation. "Okay. I'm not sorry."

"Well, you should be."

"And why is that?"

"You promised me you would sign today and so far, all we've done is talk. Take your hand off me and put it to good use."

"You're not signing either." He caught her wrist before she could send a retort. "Now behave, or I'll think you're flirting with me. Or was that your intent?"

She gave him a firm shove off the bench. "Don't hold your breath."

He smiled meaningfully. "It's only a matter of time."

"You'd better finish dressing so we can get out of here before your ego doesn't fit through the door."

Chapter Seven

Luke and Jade spent most of the afternoon walking through the tree-lined park near her condo. Being the model student, Luke made every effort to sign or spell. When they passed a jogger or a couple strolling together, he lowered his hands and waited until he and Jade were alone again. She let the incidents pass without comment. In a way she found his insecurities endearing, making him seem more human.

Often their conversations revolved around scenarios that pertained to the tapes he studied: *A Day at the Library, A Day at the Mall.*

"Most of these are useless," he complained at one point. He paused in front of a bench and motioned for her to sit down.

She sat on the wooden bench and folded her legs beneath her. "I'm sorry I don't have anything like *How to Pick up Girls,* or *A Night at the Drive-in* in my tape collection."

"Well, why not?" he asked, sliding in the seat next to her. "I think your students would find that useful."

"I teach juniors and seniors. By the time they're

79

my students, they know more about that than I do. Besides, I thought you wanted to learn how to communicate with Kyle.''

''I do. But I don't take her to the mall or the library,'' he signed.

''How about talking to her during dinner? Many of the signs carry over. Instead of learning them verbatim, practice them out of sequence. You'd be surprised at how much you already know just from being around your family.''

''The problem is not in talking to her, but in understanding her answers. She signs too fast and she won't talk while she's doing it.''

''Speech is a bone of contention with many deaf people. Almost like the French refusing to use English with the tourists.''

''I'm not a tourist in her life. I'm family.''

''A family member who doesn't use her language. Did you ever ask her to sign slower, or do you take the easy way out and look to someone else to translate?''

A guilty grin lifted the corner of his mouth. ''I take the easy way.''

''And that's why she's mad at you. You're her brother and you close her out of your life. So, she's doing the same to you.''

''I don't close her out.''

''But that's how it feels to her,'' she said sadly. ''I know, because my brother doesn't sign either.''

"You have a brother?"

She shrugged. "Yep. And a mother, too, but she went back to Portugal to live with my grandmother after my father died."

"Does your brother live around here?"

"Yes." Not that she knew where he lived or had ever been invited to his apartment, but he always managed to visit her when he needed something.

"You're not very close, are you?" Luke noted.

"His choice, not mine. I'm an embarrassment to him."

"And you figure I'm just like your brother, right?"

"Maybe I did," she admitted reluctantly. "At first."

"And now?"

"I don't." As she started to rise, Luke's hand came down on her arm. The jolt to her system was acute. The heat running through her had little to do with the outside temperature and everything to do with an internal flame. A fire that Luke inspired.

"You're not running away that easily." Luke pulled her back to the bench and wrapped his arm around her shoulders, applying a subtle pressure against her half-hearted attempt at resistance. His eyes reflected a wealth of need and longing.

Oh, great! Broad daylight in the center of a public park, he chose to turn on his charm. She couldn't say much for his timing, but his technique was certainly effective.

"I don't think . . ." His mouth brushed over hers, seriously diminishing her ability to concentrate. "This isn't the right . . ." He kissed her again. Lost in the feel of his lips caressing hers, she nearly forgot her initial reservations.

A vague flash of motion, visible from the corner of her eye, brought her back down to earth. She pressed her palms against his shoulders and wedged some distance between them. "I'm trying to say something."

With a rush of air, he expelled his frustration. "I thought we were beyond that."

"Beyond what?"

"The student/teacher or employer/employee thing, or whatever excuse you were going to make to keep this wall between us."

"Well, actually, I was going to suggest we move this some place more private. But now that you mention it . . ." She scooted off the seat before he could stop her.

Luke watched her skip down the path. A rosy flush highlighted her high cheekbones and a mass of unmanageable curls framed her face. She might have won this round but the battle was far from over.

What was it about Jade that intrigued him? He knew he affected her on a physical level. With Jade, he wanted more. But how much more? And how much of himself was he willing to give back in return?

* * *

Jade leaned across the kitchen counter and peeked into the living room. Luke hadn't moved an inch in the last half hour. Although he stared at the television, he appeared lost in thought.

Ever since their earlier kiss, he had become withdrawn. If he had regrets, why hadn't he left her at the door and gone home instead of following her inside the condo?

Men! What was the good Lord thinking when he created them?

"Coffee?" she called out.

He hit the pause button on the VCR and turned toward her. "Sorry. I guess I've been rotten company."

"Something on your mind?"

"You."

His honest answer left her momentarily speechless. She busied herself with the cups on the counter.

"No coffee," he signed, and patted the area on the sofa next to him.

Jade hesitated. She wasn't up to a replay of their tryst in the park. Something had changed. A shift in the balance of power. She couldn't deny her growing attraction for him. Evoking memories of the past no longer provided the protection she needed. Luke was not like her brother or her ex-fiancé. In fact he wasn't like any other man she had known.

She joined him in the living room, slumping into the plush cushions. In a swift, effortless movement, he scooted her next to him, cuddling one arm around her shoulders.

She tried to wriggle away, but Luke hugged her tighter, anchoring her in place. "Give it up. This way you can see me when I'm talking or signing."

She shrugged and snuggled against him. "What did you want to talk about?"

"First of all, I think I owe you money."

"I got my paycheck yesterday."

"For the teaching?"

She laughed. "I can't take money for that."

"A deal is a deal. It's business."

"How often do you kiss your business associates senseless?"

A smile lit his face. "Did I kiss you senseless?"

She scrunched her nose at him. "That's not the point."

"I know, and it doesn't change the fact that you initially took the job for the money."

"Not exactly." She had quoted him a price, figuring he would refuse. When he had called her bluff, she had been obligated to follow through. "I already get a fair paycheck from your company each week. I don't feel right taking money for the teaching when we're . . ." She struggled for the right word.

"Involved?" he supplied for her.

"I wouldn't say that," she muttered.

Luke trailed his hand across her arm. Her muscles bunched and she let out a startled gasp. Despite her reaction to his touch, she still wanted to deny the attraction. "What would you call it?"

"A mistake?"

He traced his finger along the arch of her raised eyebrow. "If it's a mistake, why are you still here?"

"I don't know."

"I think you do."

She closed her eyes to shut him out. Jade might have an effective method for ending a conversation, but he wasn't without his own weapons. He slid his hand along her neck.

Her eyes flew open wide.

"Now that I have your attention," he said.

She clasped her fingers around his wrist. "You do know how to use your hands to make a point."

His gaze focused on her face. Her eyes expressed a myriad of emotions. She wanted him, but she hesitated as if she was waiting for something more. Something he hadn't offered her thus far. A part of himself?

Apparently this beautiful, maddening woman affected more than his hormones. She stirred his emotions, too, and he wasn't sure he wanted to deal with those.

Reluctantly, he lowered his hand and cuddled her against his chest. "So, how's my signing coming along?"

"Huh?" Jade gaped at him as if he'd lost his mind. "What's wrong?"

''Besides the fact that you made a U-turn without signaling?'' Her voice broke and she swallowed hard.

''I thought that's what you wanted.''

''Five minutes ago you told me I wanted the exact opposite and then set out to prove it.'' In the long pause that followed, her expression changed from surprise to anger. ''Well, since you can't make up your mind, let me go so I can satisfy my cravings elsewhere.''

He felt as if he'd had the wind knocked out of him. ''And just where do you go to satisfy your cravings?''

''The freezer. Double fudge ice cream. Nearly as fulfilling as a man and no waiting for the phone to ring.''

It took a full ten seconds for the words to register in his brain. Enough time for Jade to wriggle out of his arms and push to her feet. He found little consolation in the fact that she looked as confused as he felt.

''You proved your point, Luke. Don't play games in the future.''

''I wasn't . . .'' he began, then realized he was speaking to her back. He followed her into the kitchen.

Before she could reach into the refrigerator, he caught her wrist and spun her around. She staggered then regained her balance, standing rigid and controlled.

He pushed a strand of hair behind her ear and left

his hand resting on her cheek. "I wasn't playing games."

She eyed him warily, inching backward until she came up against the counter. "Then why the sudden change of heart?"

"Because I wasn't being fair to you."

Her eyes widened in disbelief. "And that bothered you?"

"Yes." He raised his mouth in a half smile. Jade glared in return. "Give me a break. If I was really what you wanted right now, I wouldn't be so easily replaced by ice cream."

She lifted her shoulders in an embarrassed shrug. "I didn't say you were 'easily replaced.' And we are talking about double fudge."

"One day you'll discover there's no comparison." He lowered his head and stole a kiss from her pouting lips. She tasted far sweeter than any store-bought confection.

Her cheeks tinged pink. "Nice to see your ego hasn't suffered."

"No, not my ego. But the rest of me is suffering greatly." Luke wished she didn't look so darned pleased by his admission.

"Then I guess you want some ice cream, too?"

"Make mine a double scoop."

Jade placed the papers back in the envelope and switched off her computer. In another few weeks she would have the advance money the hospital required for her surgery. The thought filled her with hope and terror. She flopped down on her bed and propped her head up with her hands. The nagging doubts wouldn't leave her. It was a lot of money for a procedure that had only a thirty-percent chance of restoring her hearing to full capacity.

What did she hope to accomplish? She could never have a music career now, and in truth, she wouldn't give up teaching. She received too much from her students.

Strange. Just two months ago this operation had seemed so important to her. Now, she was having second thoughts. What had changed?

She glanced into the living room, where Luke was still stretched out on the floor watching a baseball game. Since she had promised to spend the day with him, he had refused to leave until the day was over. The man was persistent. Was he responsible for her confusion? Until he had pushed his way into her life, she had known exactly what she wanted and how to go about reaching her goal.

Jade rolled over to her back and stared up at the stark white ceiling. An empty ache settled in her chest. She had put her life on hold chasing a dream that might never be a reality. And for what? In the end, she would still continue to teach at the school. Her friends would still be her friends. She hadn't been working toward a goal. She had been running away from her life. Perhaps the escape she needed wasn't from her silent world but from the silence that had been left in her heart after her fiancé's desertion.

A shadow of a figure appeared on her wall. She tilted her head back to see Luke towering above her at the side of the bed. Even from upside down he posed a striking presence.

His forehead creased in an expression of concern. "Are you all right?"

"I'm just peachy."

"You don't look it."

"Thanks." She pushed herself into a sitting position.

"I was going to head home, but now I think I should stay."

"Why? So you can tell me again how lousy I look?"

He lowered himself onto the edge of the bed. The pressure of his weight caused her to slide closer to him. "I didn't say you looked lousy. You looked troubled."

"Nothing another scoop of double fudge can't cure."

"Oh. Were you pining away for me?" He grinned mischievously. "You should have called me. The game wasn't that exciting."

"You're impossible. We've never even gone on a date."

''That's your fault. You didn't want to date your boss.''

She pressed her palm against his shoulder to move him back. ''I don't want to talk about it.''

He caught her hand and laced his fingers through hers. ''Okay. Seriously. What's really troubling you?''

She would have preferred to continue with the banter. Discussing personal issues didn't come easy, a legacy of the accident that had taken her hearing. In trying to ease the guilt her family had felt, she had held her anger and fear inside.

Her smile had become a shield. If she smiled, no one saw the pain. Although she appeared to the world to be so happy, so well adjusted, she often felt so utterly alone. But not when Luke was around. So, why did she keep pushing him away?

''Answer me,'' he signed.

''I don't know what's bothering me. I thought I knew exactly what I wanted, but now I'm not sure.''

''Well, what did you think you wanted?''

''My hearing.''

''And now you don't?''

''I'd be lying if I said that. It's just not as important as I had once thought. It can't change the past or give me back what I had before the accident.''

Luke racked his brain for words of comfort. None came. He remembered the stacks of magazine articles she kept on the coffee table. Obviously she had hoped to give the new surgical procedure a try. Why the second thoughts? He wanted to ask, but worried the question might come out sounding as if he believed her to be less of a person because of her hearing deficiency.

She gazed up, her green eyes assessing him. "So, now that I've made you feel completely uncomfortable . . ."

"You didn't," he assured her, stroking the back of his hand along her cheek. "I'm just not sure how you're going to take things if I give my opinion."

"I'll take it worse if you don't give an opinion. If you have to watch every word you say, we aren't going to have much of a relationship."

He couldn't contain the grin pulling at the corner of his mouth. "I thought you weren't interested in having a relationship with me."

"That's another thing I'm not so sure about anymore. Maybe, just maybe, I was wrong about you."

"I hope it didn't cost you too much to make that admission." He cupped his hand along the back of her neck and drew her head closer, brushing a light kiss over her mouth. Her pulse raced beneath his fingertips. A whisper-soft gasp escaped from her parted lips.

"Just because I said I might have been wrong about you doesn't mean that I'm ready to go any further."

He chuckled. "There you go again. Don't you know what they say about protesting too much? Besides, we're sitting on your bed."

She glanced around the room as if she hadn't been aware of their intimate surroundings before. A crimson blush flooded her face. She scrambled off the edge of the bed, dropping her feet to the floor with a thud.

Luke let out a laugh. Although the surroundings offered intriguing possibilities, he would gain more by waiting. With her personal revelations of today still fresh in his mind, he couldn't take advantage of her temporarily fragile state.

"Don't think it will be that easy," Jade said as if reading his mind. Her voice vibrated with challenge.

"Meaning?"

She raised her head slowly. A halo of curls framed her face. She stared intensely, her eyes reflecting all the fire of the jewels they resembled. Gone was the shyness that had prevailed only seconds before. Her full pink lips lifted in a mystical smile.

"It's gonna cost you, too, and I don't mean money."

Her smile was beguiling, bewitching, and exceedingly frightening to a man who had managed to successfully avoid emotional attachments. Now he knew how Faust felt, for her devilish warning implied that she expected no less than a piece of his soul.

Chapter Eight

"You're uncharacteristically quiet today, Luke."

Robert's taunt invaded the uneasy musing that had plagued Luke most of the morning. The surprise invitation from his mother to join the family for Sunday brunch had seemed like an ideal way to escape his conflicting thoughts. Instead, he found his mind wandering more often than not.

"Sorry," Luke signed and answered at the same time. About the only good that had come out of his visit was Kyle's positive response to his progress in signing.

"Woman troubles?" Robert asked.

Kyle giggled, a sound he couldn't ever remember hearing. "What woman would want him?" she signed, and even mouthed the words at the same time to make sure her brother caught her teasing.

"Thank you for that helpful suggestion." He grinned, feeling mighty pleased with his ability to hold his own.

"Is that one from *A Day at the Mall*?" Robert asked.

"No. *A Day at the Library,*" Vivian added with a trace of humor.

Oddly, Kyle jumped to his defense, her eyes and hands conveying her displeasure. "If you make fun of him, he'll stop trying."

"No I won't," Luke told her.

Kyle's smile mirrored her relief. "You're getting so good that soon you'll be able to pick up deaf girls."

Luke choked on his coffee. "Excuse me?"

"Obviously the ones that can hear you keep their distance." He never realized that his sister was quite the little jokester. "After Mom leaves, I'll teach you how to curse."

"No, thank you," Luke replied, trying to look stern. He had a feeling those kinds of signs were easily learned from Jade if she was mad enough.

"Why?" Kyle signed.

Vivian raised her hands and said, "Stop trying to shock your brother, and behave like a lady. Start by clearing the table."

Luke held back a laugh at the contorted faces Kyle made when her mother wasn't looking. He wondered how many of those glaring expressions had been directed at him over the years. Maybe he was better off not knowing.

"So, you've been spending a lot of time with Jade," Robert noted when they were alone. "Your signing has improved dramatically."

"I never realized how much I already knew. I just didn't feel comfortable trying to use it."

"Well, it's done a world of good for Kyle."

"It appears so," he muttered absently.

"Then what's your problem?"

"Who says I have one?"

His cousin raised his coffee cup in a mock toast. "Have it your way. But if I had to guess, I'd say it has something to do with Jade."

"I don't have a problem with Jade." Unless, of course, he wanted to count the serious case of cowardice he had suddenly developed.

Yesterday he had thwarted her every attempt to keep their relationship professional. He argued, and very persuasively, that they should explore the undeniable attraction between them. Convinced he knew better, he dismissed her misgivings as excuses. Yet, it only took one small demand—that he give as much of himself as he expected from her—to send him running. Maybe not literally, but emotionally.

"Are you sure you know what you're doing, Luke?"

"Is it necessary to know?" he wondered aloud.

"Maybe not. And in your case, it might be an advantage."

"Meaning?"

"You rarely do anything without a purpose. Where Jade is concerned, I'd hate to think you were using her. I like her."

Did Robert also harbor a crush on the beautiful teacher? He had known Jade a lot longer. Luke didn't want to unwittingly hurt his cousin. "Let me ask you something, Robert."

"Dating advice?" Robert joked and grinned.

"When I have to ask advice from a kid, ten years my junior, I'll get out of the dating game."

Robert chuckled. "Okay, old man. What did you want to know?"

"Does it bother you that I'm seeing Jade?"

"Would you stop seeing her if I said yes?"

"No," Luke said.

"Then it doesn't bother me."

"Care to explain that logic?"

"If you had said yes, it would have meant you really didn't care about her, and that would have bothered me."

Luke stretched to alleviate the tightness that had seeped into his limbs. Of course he cared about Jade. He hadn't yet become as impersonal and cold as his computer. But was he being fair to her? Could he give her what she needed? Did he even understand what she needed?

He could write volumes on what he knew about the mail-order business, but he couldn't fill a paragraph on what he knew about women. Couple that with his total ignorance of her world and he had to admit, Jade had been right. He had expected a very one-sided relationship. One where she did all the compromising.

* * *

Jade coasted down the suburban street at a steady pace. The tall oaks and maple trees that lined the road made her feel as if she were traveling through a long leafy archway. A haze rose from the black asphalt as the sun burned off the remains of a morning shower.

For Jade, Rollerblading was more than exercise. She enjoyed the freedom of cruising along with the wind blowing through her hair. A working girl's convertible, she jokingly called her skates.

Many of her neighbors also made use of the hot day. She steered herself through a spray of cool water, where two young kids were washing their parents' car. Around the next bend she managed to catch the fringes of a sprinkler, watering a lush green lawn.

On her third trip around the quiet neighborhood, she stopped at a convenience store and picked up the Sunday *Hartford Courant,* then headed for home. Her chores were still not done. She frowned. Luke had hung around the entire day yesterday, keeping her from the housework, yet he bolted fast enough the moment she had hinted at that horrifying concept of mutual commitment.

She shouldn't be surprised, but for some reason she was. Had she expected him to be different, more understanding because of his sister? She should be grateful he decided to turn tail now instead of after she became any more involved.

Wiping away the perspiration that had beaded on

her forehead, she skated the last half block to her condo. With the newspaper clutched tightly against her chest, she sprinted up the sidewalk. Who needed a man anyway? They were nothing but trouble.

She brought herself to a screeching halt only inches before barreling into Luke, who was standing on her front landing. He raised his hands reflexively to her waist, steadying her in his strong embrace. His startled, wide-eyed gaze locked with hers and her heart fluttered. An unexpected surge of heat coursed through her, awakening the emotions she had spent the last hour trying to repress.

Who needed a man? They're nothing but trouble, a little voice mocked in her ear.

"Oh, shut up," she muttered.

"What?" Luke asked.

"Nothing. I was talking to myself. What are you doing here?"

"I told you I'd be back today."

She twisted out of the arms that encircled her and rolled backward. "Oh, right. Was that before or after you nearly tripped over yourself in your haste to leave last night?" She dropped onto the wrought-iron bench.

"I wasn't in a hurry last night." He bent down, cupped her leg with one hand, and pulled off her skate. "You know, you should wear knee pads and elbow pads when you're doing this."

"Who appointed you my guardian?"

"Obviously, you need a keeper. You should wear

your hearing aid, too, so you can hear any car horn trying to warn you.''

She shot him a scathing glare that had no effect.

''Give me the other foot.''

Lifting up the heavy boot, she allowed him to finish playing his paternal role. Not that there was anything fatherly about the way his hungry gaze appraised her legs as he worked. And there was nothing familial about the way he massaged the back of her calf, trailing down to the ankle and finally the bottom of her foot.

Her grip tightened around the paper still pressed against her chest. She never realized that her toes could experience such pleasure. Any residual anger receded to the farthest corner of her mind.

''Luke,'' she choked out.

''Yes?''

She tried not to take notice of his self-satisfied grin. He had every right to be cocky. Just one touch and she had crumbled. ''Can we move this inside?''

''I thought you were mad at me.''

''Well, apparently, you didn't let it bother you too much.''

''It's my way of apologizing.''

If this was his idea of an apology then she hoped he was wrong more often.

Luke extended his hand and pulled her to her shaky legs. Before she saw it coming, he covered her mouth in a long, lingering kiss.

Surprise quickly turned to delight. She raised to the tips of her bare feet, slipping one arm across his shoulder for support. The gentle teasing of his lips filled her with anticipation, and more than a little impatience.

Luke's hand slid across her back but further progress was hampered by the *Hartford Courant* wedged firmly between their bodies. Slowly, with a grunt of exasperation, he drew back.

"Lady, you could test the vows of a monk."

She laughed as she pulled at the front cover of the newspaper that stuck to her bare arms. "If you're thinking of becoming one, you're going about it the wrong way."

"I only meant this wasn't what I had intended." She raised an eyebrow and he quickly added, "Yet."

Jade removed the key from her pocket and inserted it in the lock. "I wasn't sure you would come back today."

He nodded. "I wasn't either."

A blast of air-conditioning hit her as she stepped inside the condo. She dropped the paper on the hall table and followed Luke into the living room. He lowered himself into the recliner and folded his arms across his chest. The gesture accentuated the powerful muscles beneath his fitted rugby shirt, but left him looking less than relaxed.

"Why are you here?"

"I had brunch with my family today."

She sat on the arm of the chair and placed a comforting hand on his tense shoulder. "Things didn't go well, I guess?"

He shook his head. "Actually, they went great. I had a pleasant conversation with Kyle."

"She spoke?"

"Well, not exactly. More like mouthing the words while she signed, but that's more of a response than I've gotten in years."

"So what does that have to do with me?"

"Everything." He tugged on a belt loop of her jeans and caught her around the waist as she tumbled into his lap. She ran her fingers through her damp tangle of curls. "I have to take a shower."

"Later. I need to clear up a few things."

Now he wanted to talk? Now, while she felt sticky and grimy and definitely at a disadvantage? "Can't it wait a few minutes?"

"No."

"Okay." She tilted her head and waited for him to continue.

For the first time she actually wondered how he sounded. Did his voice have a deep rich timbre, as she imagined? She laid her fingers against the base of his throat.

"What are you doing?" he asked.

"I want to see what your voice feels like. Just ignore me. Go ahead and talk."

Luke inhaled deeply. Ignore her? Only if he stopped breathing.

He had rehearsed his speech in the car on the ride over. The words now seemed inadequate. How would he convince her that he could be more understanding of her needs when her small gesture had thrown him off balance?

"So, what was so important it couldn't wait?" she asked.

Luke blurted out the first thing that came to his mind. "I have to attend a dinner engagement next weekend. Would you like to go with me?"

She wriggled her nose in distaste. "You waited until I look and feel like an old mop to ask me on a date?"

"You look fine to me."

Jade rolled her eyes. "Business dinner?"

"Yes."

Her face clouded over and she dropped her hand into her lap. "I wouldn't be much of a business asset for you."

"What's that supposed to mean?"

"You're liable to make your colleagues uncomfortable."

"Who told you that?" Although she didn't answer, he could guess. She must have been hurt very badly by an ignorant and unfeeling man. "I doubt my colleagues will care either way."

"Then why have you never let Kyle act as hostess for one of your business functions when she asked?"

"How do you know I haven't?"

"Have you?" Her eyebrow arched in challenge.

"No."

Her mouth lifted in a sad smile. "It's obvious by the way you keep your family life separate from everything else."

"You still believe you can keep your life in neat little compartments." Robert's words came back to haunt him.

"It wasn't a conscious decision. My mother was barely coping with the loss of her husband. Kyle needed special schools, and that took money. I gave up my dreams and devoted all my time to the company to get it back on its feet. My dad was a great guy but as a businessman, he lacked the killer instinct."

"And you had it?"

"Maybe not at nineteen when I inherited the mess my father had left, but by twenty, you can believe I learned."

"You're not twenty anymore."

"No, I'm not." He marveled at how she had taken the focus off herself by putting him on the defensive. She didn't verbally attack. She was more like the subtle voice of conscience. "But you get into a way of life and it becomes difficult to change. Maybe it was selfish to expect Kyle to make my life easier by talking instead of expecting me to sign, I just didn't see it at the time.''

"Did you ever tell Kyle any of this?''

"To make her feel guilty?''

"To help her understand.''

"And what about you, Jade? Do you tell your own brother how hurt you are that he never learned to sign?''

Her body went rigid. "That's different.''

Resentment flared in him. He was tired of paying for someone else's mistakes. "Why? You defend Kyle's right to resent me for not learning yet you didn't require that your brother learn.''

"They're two different cases.'' She sucked in a large gulp of air, as if to steady the shakiness in her voice. Apparently he had touched a raw nerve.

"How?''

Her gaze rested on some distant point. Only his arm wrapped firmly around her waist stopped her from scrambling out of the chair.

Cupping his hand over her chin, he forced her to look at him. "How is it different?''

For a long moment she didn't reply. Her rounded eyes took on an icy glare that made her seem coldly detached. When she finally spoke, pain vibrated in her words. "Because you love your sister, and my brother hates me.''

Luke's anger dissipated. That was the one argument

he couldn't answer. For the first time in his life, he understood what it meant to be at a loss for words.

He pushed his fingers into the mass of curls at her temple and gently urged her head to rest on his shoulder. She curled against him. Her warm breath caressed his neck.

Her very presence was exquisite. He stifled a groan.

The idea is to lend comfort, he told himself. *Ignore the way she's making you crazy. She doesn't know what she's doing.*

Chapter Nine

Jade tried to ignore the persistent tapping on her arm. Far too comfortable to leave the source of warmth and protection surrounding her, she pushed the annoying hand away. A deep rumbling vibrated against her ear. She opened her eyes and gazed into Luke's laughing face.

"You don't like to wake up, do you?"

"No."

"You have company."

"You're not company." She stretched her cramped limbs. Disoriented, she glanced around the room to get her bearings. After a few foggy seconds, she noticed the flashing lights and understood his meaning. "I'd better see who's at the door," she mumbled, and scooted off the chair.

A quick glance at her watch told her she'd been asleep for over an hour. How had that happened? The last thing she remembered was trying her hardest to crack Luke's single-minded control. At what point had a flirtation turned into a nap? An embarrassed flush washed over her. She must be more inexperienced than she'd thought.

The lights flashed again. She raked her hand through her tousled hair hoping to restore some order before facing her visitor. The gesture was futile.

She opened the door. Her brother's grinning face greeted her and she let out a groan. The edge of a gold Mylar box stuck out from under his arm.

"I hope the other guy looks worse," Anton said of her disheveled appearance. By contrast, he looked as if he had stepped off the pages of *Gentleman's Quarterly*.

"Thanks."

"May I come in?" he asked, then pushed his way in without waiting for an answer.

What did he want? she wondered. He couldn't need money again already. "What are you doing here?"

His eyes narrowed. "Last week you told me I never visit unless I want something. Well, here I am."

Anton swaggered into the room, but stopped short when he caught sight of Luke's imposing frame leaning against the kitchen counter. Luke eyed her brother like a stag about to take to battle in a territorial dispute. If she wasn't still feeling the residual effect of sleep she might have appreciated the humor of the situation.

"You should have told me you had company," her brother said.

"Like you gave me a chance," she said and shrugged. "Luke, this is my brother, Anton."

Luke's eyes flashed with surprise, then narrowed as he offered his hand. "A pleasure."

"So you finally dumped the lawyer," Anton noted as he shook Luke's outstretched hand. "About time. The guy was a loser."

On that note, Jade would agree, but Anton's reasons had nothing to do with his sister's welfare. Her ex-fiancé had often interfered when Anton wanted money from her. "We split up last year, but thanks for noticing."

An awkward silence followed.

"Oh, here." Anton offered her a box that had been tucked under his arm. "Happy Birthday."

"Thanks." Her fingers tightened around the edge of the present.

"Go on. Open it."

She tugged at the taped edges of the store-wrapped gift. Inside was a box of chocolate-covered strawberries. She forced a smile. "Thanks. You shouldn't have."

"Oh, come on. I had a good week."

Luke stood next to Jade and took her hand in his. The gesture, although possessive, still allowed her the needed space to see both men while they spoke. "What do you do, Anton?" he asked.

"Oh . . . I guess you could say I'm an investment broker."

"Securities? Bonds? Commodities?"

Horses, Jade thought as Anton babbled on, trying to sound impressive on a subject he knew nothing about.

He had come on his own, and he didn't want money. She shouldn't question her luck, but somehow, she didn't trust him. He wanted something but he wouldn't ask in Luke's presence.

"I'll get some coffee," she said. Not that either man took notice. She spent the next half hour in the kitchen while Anton and Luke did the male bonding thing over the baseball game. Was she jealous that her brother developed an easy rapport with Luke yet had trouble spending five minutes in her presence?

Only when Anton left could she relax again. She closed the door and exhaled a sigh of relief. Luke came up in front of her and leaned against the wall with his solid frame.

"You've been very quiet. Why?"

"I can't join in the conversation if you don't look at me when you're speaking."

He winced. "I'm sorry."

"You weren't the one who was deliberately leaving me out. Then again, I don't know why I'm surprised."

Luke's expression changed to one of concern. "Don't you think you're being too hard on him? He's young . . ."

"He's older than me."

"All right. He's immature. But he obviously cares

more than you realize. He brought you a birthday present, making me feel like a rot since I didn't know.''

She shook her head sorrowfully. ''It's not my birthday. Not even close.''

''Oh. Well, men aren't always good with dates.''

''When is Kyle's birthday?''

By his guilty frown, she would bet he knew the exact date. ''Bad example. But he did buy a gift. And I know you love chocolate.''

''But I'm allergic to strawberries, which he knows because he used to delight in making fun of me when I'd break out in a rash.''

''I think you're looking to find fault . . .''

Jade smacked her palms into his shoulder and pushed him back. ''I should have known you'd take his side.''

''I'm not taking sides.''

''Of course not,'' she said with saccharine sweetness. ''You're just offering some helpful advice because after a one-hour conversation you would naturally know my brother and his motives better than I do.''

As she tried to walk away, he caught her wrist in his steel grip. ''Look, I know there's more going on here than a forgotten birthday. What's really bothering you?''

''There's sixteen years of history going on here, and your armchair analysis isn't going to solve our problems in one afternoon.'' She glared at his fingers wrapped tightly around her wrist. "Let go, please. I want to take a shower."

Luke paced the floor of the living room. Why was Jade so prickly and irritable? He suppressed a chuckle. She would likely inflict physical damage if he called her that now.

He thought back to her brother's visit. Anton *had* positioned himself in a way that directed all conversation away from his sister. Luke thought about his own relationship with Kyle. Although he hadn't been able to sign either, he had never ignored her when she was in the same room.

Sixteen years of history. Jade had lost her hearing in an accident sixteen years ago. What was the correlation between that accident and the demise of their sibling relationship? Tragedy usually brought a family closer.

The jingle of keys disrupted his train of thought. Jade had finished her shower and changed into a pair of leggings and an oversized T-shirt that had *The Rolling Stones* emblazoned on the front. Her damp hair sprung into ringlets around her face. She reached for her purse from the hall table.

"Where are you going?" he signed.

"Out," she signed. Her hands moved in a stiff, jerking motion. "Are you coming?"

"Do you want me to?"

She shrugged as if she didn't care either way. "Do you want to drive or should I?"

"You drive?"

Her eyes flashed with indignation and she reverted to speech. "Why wouldn't I?"

He crossed the room in three easy strides and stood in front of her. "Don't get defensive. I'm not the one you're angry with. You take the bus to work, so I assumed you didn't own a car. Shoot me!"

"I take the bus because it's environmentally friendly and I hate driving to the city during rush hour." She paused, then hunched her shoulders in apology. "And I'm not mad at you. I'm jealous."

He couldn't hide his surprise at her painfully honest admission. "Why?"

"Because Anton had more to say to you this afternoon than he's had to say to me in the last year."

"I could say the same about Kyle."

"That doesn't make it hurt less."

"I know." He kissed her forehead. "So where do you want to go?"

"I have to go food shopping. My refrigerator is empty."

"I'll take you to dinner."

"That's very generous, but I still have to eat the rest of the week."

"All right, the supermarket." He slipped his arm around her waist and gazed into her eyes. "When we get back, you can tell me all about the lawyer."

"The lawyer," she repeated. Her body went rigid. Evidently he had stumbled on another touchy subject. "That is not open for discussion."

"Why?"

"For a man who volunteers nothing about himself, you have a morbid curiosity about my life."

Luke had to admit his fascination with her was out of character. The intricate facets that made up Jade's personality drew a detailed portrait of the triumph of spirit. He admired her strength, respected her fierce independence. She reminded him a lot of himself.

"My interest in you is not morbid," he said as he opened the door.

"Then what would you call it?"

"I'd call it ironic. A punishment that fits the crime."

"And what are you guilty of, Luke?"

"Ignorance." Ignorance of a world and culture he should have known as well as his own.

"Don't try to overcompensate by taking on too much. Some facts aren't relevant, so butt out of my past."

Jade might not want to discuss the man, but Luke got the impression that the lawyer was very relevant, both in the way she viewed herself and the way she perceived him.

Jade folded her arms on the desk and laid her head on top. Tension rippled across her shoulders. She had never been so happy for a week to end. Particularly this one. The bizarre events of the past few days made her wonder if she had fallen into the middle of a surrealistic novel. To say that Luke had been acting strange would be a gross understatement.

Was he upset because she had refrained from boring him with the details of her broken engagement? She hadn't asked him for an account of all the women in his past. Evidently, something was bothering him. Every evening he had come to her condo after work, but she could have been a stranger for all the affection he showed her. The biggest joke of all was that he had insisted *she* sign everything.

Whenever she had tried to snuggle close to him, he found a polite yet firm way to extract himself. "I'm here to learn," he had claimed.

While she found his attitude mildly amusing on Monday, by Thursday, his tantrum had begun to wear thin.

Men were such babies when they didn't get their way. She groaned in annoyance.

A tap on her shoulder sent her bolting upright. She swiveled her chair and gazed up into Robert's smiling face.

"Are they working you too hard? Complain to the boss."

"The boss is the one who's working me too hard. Every night..." She paused when Robert's mouth turned up in a humorous smirk.

"Go on. Every night, what?"

"Not what you're thinking." She wasn't sure what Luke had hoped to prove, but he was driving her crazy. "He's decided to become the student of the year."

"And this disappoints you?"

"Well, no . . ."

"Luke is like that. Once he decides he wants something, he doesn't stop until he's reached his goal."

"Oh, great," she grumbled. Just what had Luke set as his goal? Hadn't she already offered him what he wanted?

He didn't strike her as the sensitive, sharing type. If anything, he seemed to be more of a loner, who preferred not to know about the emotional baggage the people around him carried.

"Think of the money you're making," Robert said, dragging her away from her thoughts.

"I can't take his money. . . ."

"I knew it." He grinned as if he'd won the lottery. "You two are perfectly suited."

"And how did you come up with that brilliant theory?"

"You both put all your energies into running other people's lives so you don't have to deal with your own. And right about now you're probably locking horns over who is going to run whose life."

She laughed. "This is what happens when you take a pop psychology course. You start to add two and two together and come up with five. Although you could be right about Luke.''

''You, too, Teach. I've seen how involved you become with your students.''

''Are you referring to Luke?''

''No, but he's a good example of how you interfered for his own good. The effect on his relationship with Kyle is remarkable. And all this because you pushed him into it.''

She exhaled a disgusted grunt. ''Get a life, Robert.''

''Why should I when you and Luke provide me with so much entertainment?'' He ruffled her hair. ''Have a good weekend.''

''Yeah, sure,'' she grumbled to his retreating back. She rose and reached for her purse from the desk. Would Luke show up again this evening? Did she want him to?

After settling her sunglasses on the bridge of her nose, Jade stepped into the warm afternoon air. Traffic whizzed by, most people anxious to leave the city and begin their long, Fourth of July weekend. She thought about taking a trip to the beach herself tomorrow, then remembered she was supposed to go on a date with the same man who had been quietly tormenting her all week. Would he continue to treat her as his employee?

On the short walk to the bus stop, she noticed a sleek black car pull up to the curb. Her first instinct was to quicken her pace, until she recognized the three-pointed star hood ornament on Luke's Mercedes.

The passenger window opened. Jade leaned down to glance inside the car.

"Need a ride?" he asked.

She pushed her glasses to the top of her head. "The bus will be here soon."

"Do you *want* a ride?"

"Sure, why not?"

He leaned across the console and opened her door. "Hop in."

She slid into the seat. Once settled, she deliberately showed off her legs by slightly hiking her navy blue skirt above her knees. If she failed to get a reaction, she would write him off as a human computer and give up.

Luke checked the side-view mirror before pulling into the flow of traffic. She knew how to make a point! His gaze wandered again to the sleek, stocking-clad leg that dangled restlessly over the other one.

In an act of desperation, he turned the air-conditioning to full power. The blast of cold air didn't help. He tossed his jacket over her knees.

Jade broke out in a satisfied grin. "Something wrong?"

"I wouldn't want you to catch a chill."

"How considerate of you." Her green eyes shimmered with amusement.

He focused his attention on driving.

After a half hour of silence, he felt Jade's fingers tighten around his arm. "You missed the exit."

"I didn't miss it. We're going to my place."

"What?"

"My house," he spelled out rather than look at her again.

"Oh, fine," she said simply.

Her cool, indifferent manner made him seethe. Those two qualities of hers that he had admired last week—her strength and her independence—were now driving him to distraction.

Luke slammed his palm against the steering wheel. He wasn't used to dealing with a woman who didn't want or need anything from him. Particularly a woman who provoked such strong protective instincts. His intention had always been to shelter those he cared about and keep them safe. Unfortunately, he had never found the right balance between helping and controlling.

Chapter Ten

Jade settled herself into the corner of the sofa. She couldn't get over the transformation that had taken place in Luke's apartment in one short week. The large wooden furnishings hadn't changed, but the walls, now stark white, made the room seem twice as big. The smell of fresh paint lingered.

She kicked off her shoes and tucked her legs beneath her. With a weary sigh, she rested her head against the arm of the sofa. Outside a storm raged but it was nothing compared to the turbulent emotions raging inside her. What kind of game was Luke playing now? In the two hours she had been there, he hadn't asked her anything more personal than "salt or pepper?"

He had cooked dinner, a beef stir-fry that was surprisingly good. While they ate, he watched the evening news until, in anger, she snapped off the television. Through the rest of the meal, he remained silent. Did he bring her home just so he could ignore her?

Luke came into the room, carrying a tray with two steaming mugs. He had changed into a pair of sweatpants that rode low on his hips and a sleeveless sweat-shirt that exposed his well-defined biceps and triceps. As an attention grabber, it ranked right up there with hiking her skirt up above the knee. Luke knew how to even the score.

The aroma of fresh coffee and the deliciously masculine scent of Luke provided a feast for her senses. He handed a cup to her.

"Thank you."

"You're welcome." His clipped answer let her know he wasn't planning to serve up any conversation with the coffee. She would have to drag words out of him syllable by syllable.

"The room looks great," she said.

"Thanks."

"You really did a lot of work in a short time."

"Yes." He lowered himself into a chair with lazy ease.

"I like the new rug. Is it Persian?"

"Yes."

"Okay." She sprung from the seat and slipped her feet inside her leather pumps. "I've enjoyed about as much of this as I can stand. Would you be so kind as to call me a cab?"

His brown eyes rounded innocently. "Have I done something to offend you?"

"No. You've been a perfect gentleman."

"Then what's wrong?"

"Do you have a phone book?"

His expression changed to one of concern. The man should have been an actor. "You seem agitated."

"A washing machine agitates. I'm ticked off."

"Why?"

"I'm sure you're enjoying yourself immensely, but I've taken as much of your temper tantrum as I'm going to."

"I don't know what you're talking about."

"Yes you do. You've been ignoring me all week."

"I've been at your house every night, Jade," he reminded her.

"Someone kept showing up. Roboman, I believe. The human computer."

"You are one tough lady to please."

She gaped at him in disbelief. "How would you know? You didn't make an effort."

His laughter sent her temper soaring.

"Do you have a phone book or not?" she asked.

"Why are you angry? I'm only doing what you asked me to do."

"Oh, this should be good." She folded her arms across her chest. "How do you figure that?"

"You told me to stay out of your life."

"When?"

" 'Some facts aren't relevant so butt out of my past,' " he mimicked her words.

"Past being the operative word, Luke. Not my life, my *past*."

He shook his head. "Same thing. They're connected."

"Let me get this straight. Because *you've* decided my past is relevant, a relationship is out of the question between us until I tell you about the men in my life? I don't recall your being all that concerned the first time you flirted with me."

His jaw clenched. Apparently, he didn't like to hear the truth. "That's not what I meant."

"Forget it. I'm not so hard up that I have to debate a man on why he should have a relationship with me. When you want to talk this out like an adult, you know where to find me." She sprinted across the room. "Never mind about the phone book. I'll get a cab on the street."

She bolted out the door and slammed it shut behind her. As she pushed the button for the elevator, she swore silently under her breath.

Men! Borrow one lousy rib from them during Creation and they think they can make us pay for eternity. She pushed the button again. "Oh, come on. Pay this much for rent and you ought to get an elevator before Christmas."

A breeze swirled around her legs. She glanced over her shoulder to see Luke walking down the hall. He gave her one of those smiles that set her pulse racing. Anger mingled with excitement, bringing a warm flush to her cheeks. A man that attractive should be locked away in a cell, not turned loose on an unsuspecting female population.

He came up behind her and slipped his arms around her waist. Why did he have to feel so good? Her attempt to wiggle free was halfhearted at best.

"You're such a child," she grumbled.

He turned her around and hugged her against his rock-solid body. She could feel the power and strength of him. He was completely male.

She started to reach back when the elevator doors swung open wide. Startled, she froze. Thankfully, the elevator was empty. A nervous giggle escaped. She turned in the circle of Luke's arms and clasped her hands over his shoulders.

"Don't leave yet. It's pouring outside," he said.

She pressed in closer. "Are you going to continue to ignore me if we go back inside?"

"I doubt that's possible," he said with what appeared to be great difficulty.

"Then what do you want?"

"Darned if I know. This is untouched territory for me."

Her eyebrow arched in question. "Oh, really?"

"You're so literal."

"Most deaf people are. I can't hear your tone of voice so I have to trust my other senses. What I see . . ." She traced a finger over his furrowed brow. "What I taste . . ." She kissed his mouth. "And what I feel." Her hand slid over his chest.

His body jerked in response. "Do you know what you're doing to me?"

"I sure do," she muttered in his ear. "I'm paying you back for ignoring me all week."

"I didn't like being told to butt out of your life. I reacted badly and I'm sorry."

"It wasn't all your fault. I should have just answered the question."

"Does that mean you'll answer next time?"

"That depends on when and why you ask."

He led her back into the living room and joined her on the sofa. Despite her attempts to find a position that gave her better leverage, she could do no more than snuggle alongside him. He laced his fingers tightly through hers, she suspected, to stop her errant hand from testing the fragile control he just barely managed to maintain. Tomorrow she would probably thank him for his display of self-control. Logically, she knew her emotions were too jumbled for her to think straight.

He pressed a kiss against her cheek. "Would you at least try to behave? You're skating on thin ice here."

"You should have let me go home when you had the chance. In fact, I should get going while there's a slight lull in the storm." She made no attempt to move. The feeling of him close to her, the warmth that he supplied, was too comforting to leave in spite of her words to the contrary.

"It's pretty bad out there. Stay here tonight."

She gazed into his eyes. "I really shouldn't . . ."

"I have a guest room."

"I didn't bring anything with—" Her excuse was cut off by a long, deep kiss.

"I'm sure I can find you something to sleep in."

Against her better judgment, she found herself agreeing. Why bother trying to deny what she felt? She was in too deep to back out now. The man had a hold on her heart so tight, she might never be free. He must care for her. Why else would he have put on the brakes before their relationship became too hot to handle, yet treat her so tenderly?

"Come on. We'll find you something more comfortable to slip into before you have a chance to change your mind."

She followed him into his bedroom. While he rooted through the walk-in closet, she sat down on the edge of the king-size bed. The decor, so utterly masculine, complemented Luke to perfection. She stared up at the ceiling, feeling dwarfed by the room.

The first indication that Luke had returned came when his shadow fell across her. She raised her head to find him staring at her.

She pushed quickly to her feet, and he pulled her into his arms. She felt a rumble of laughter vibrating against his chest as he tugged her to him. "You are going to be the death of me."

Without hearing the inflection in his voice, she couldn't tell if he was joking. Not for the first time she wondered what he sounded like—when he was teasing her or angry with her and especially when he spoke from the heart. That was one tone of voice she might never know.

A lump formed in her throat. The last thing she wanted to do was get weepy and sentimental in front of Luke.

"I need the bathroom." She scooted past him, grabbing the sweatshirt from his hand as she darted down the corridor.

Jade stepped inside the large bathroom and padded across the red and black ceramic tiles to the sink. After stripping off her clothes, she splashed cold water over her arms and face, hoping to shock herself out of the blue funk that had overcome her. It didn't help. He obviously felt something for her, and he was willing to wait as long as it took to win her trust completely. So why was she hiding in the bathroom feeling sorry for herself?

She pulled the sweatshirt on, smoothing the soft fleece over her hips. The sandalwood scent of his after-shave still lingered. If she weren't so overly proud she would wear her hearing aid. Luke wouldn't treat her differently. Would he?

The door opened and Luke stepped inside. She raised her head to glance at him in the mirror. He hunched his shoulders apologetically. "I knocked first."

"That's okay. I'd be a hypocrite if I acted all shy and outraged now. Did you need the bathroom?"

"I came to check on you."

"I'm fine."

"Then why are you hanging out in here?"

She glanced around the large room and waved her hand in a sweeping motion. "A glass-encased shower and a pool-sized bathtub. I was deciding where to begin."

The slight tilt of his head said he didn't believe her. "Start with the truth and then you can try out the Jacuzzi."

At the warning glint in his eye, a snappy comeback died on her lips. One minute she was flirting outrageously and the next she had taken a cowardly retreat. Certainly, he deserved some answers. She leaned against the tile counter and crossed her arms over her chest. "You'll probably think this sounds selfish."

"I won't," he said and nodded for her to continue.

"Before the accident, I lived in a world of music. My parents bragged incessantly about their musical prodigy. There was even talk of my playing Carnegie Hall. And I liked the attention."

He shrugged. "There's nothing wrong with that."

Jade closed her eyes, as if she could block out the memory of that fateful day. Her body shuddered. While the explosion had thrown her clear of the ensuing fire, her auditory nerves had suffered irreversible damage. At least until the recent developments in medical technology.

"When the doctors told my parents that I might never hear again, nothing was ever the same. I didn't just lose my hearing. I lost my family."

"How?"

An aching emptiness engulfed her. "Anton was quite brilliant in his own way. He loved science, even built himself a lab in the basement. But he was a kid, and easily distracted. He went out to play baseball with some friends without properly shutting down his equipment."

"I can figure out the rest," Luke said.

"My mother and father never let Anton forget that his carelessness had caused the accident. And, although I never blamed my brother, I think he hated me anyway."

"He probably didn't know how to deal with the guilt laid on him by your parents."

Jade raked her fingers through her hair. "None of my family seemed to be able to adjust. Deaf culture made them nervous. A constant reminder of how radically their lives had changed."

"Your life had changed, not theirs."

"Everyone was affected. I tried to pretend that I didn't care. That the music wasn't that important to me. I never used Sign Language in front of my family. I still don't."

Luke stepped closer. "All right. But what does that have to do with here and now?"

"Most of the time I don't dwell on the past. But sometimes I really miss the music and the sounds. Especially around you. When you talk I want . . . I mean . . . I wonder what—" At the guilty expression on Luke's face, Jade cut off her words. Blinking back the tears that filled her eyes, she raised her hands in a gesture of futility. "Every man's worst nightmare. A woman who gets sappy and emotional."

"I don't mind."

"I told you it would sound selfish."

"You're being too hard on yourself. You are entitled to get angry sometimes." He hooked his thumb in the neck of the sweatshirt and drew her nearer. "As for what I sound like, you're not missing much. Just look at the way my employees cringe when I ask to speak with them."

Her laugh mingled with a hiccup. She imagined his voice was every bit as attractive as the rest of him. "You're just trying to make me feel better."

"Is it working?"

"Yes." She smiled. How could she not when he gazed at her with such concern? Luke shouldn't be made to regret his ability to hear just because she couldn't.

"Why don't you get some sleep? You'll feel better in the morning."

"I might be less emotional, but will I still be my fantastic, usual self?" she joked.

He raised an eyebrow. "We'll have to find out to-morrow."

"Well, then, I'll hit the sack right away. The sooner I get to sleep the sooner I'll wake up." She popped a kiss on his cheek and skipped down the hall toward the guest room.

Chapter Eleven

Luke hovered in the doorway of the study. He towel-dried his hair while he listened to Jade play some vintage Elton John tunes on the piano. With her hair pulled back in a ponytail, he could see her hearing aid. Why did she refuse to wear the device around him? Only last night she had admitted to missing the sounds in her life, yet she resisted using the one thing that could help her. Was she really treated differently when she wore her hearing aid? In this age of political correctness, he felt sure that people were more sensitive than they used to be.

When she finished playing, he stepped inside the room. The moment she saw him, her hand went automatically to her ear.

"Leave it in," he said.

She shook her head.

"Why?" he asked.

"It'll make you uncomfortable."

"Did it make *the lawyer* uncomfortable?"

Although he could have shot himself for blurting out the accusation in that manner, she didn't appear to

131

be upset. "I wondered when you would get to him. Yes, he did prefer that I leave the hearing aid at home when we went out. As a matter of fact, toward the end, he usually preferred to leave *me* at home when he went out."

"I'm not him and I don't care either way."

She arched an eyebrow in question. "If you're so blasé about this whole thing, then why don't you sign while you're talking? Particularly when we're in public."

"You're right," he signed and spoke simultaneously. "So I'll sign today, and you'll wear the hearing aid all day."

She shrugged in agreement. "I'll wear it until we leave for the dinner party tonight."

"All day and into the night." He sat next to her on the bench. Her long, bare legs peeked from under the soft cotton sweatshirt she wore. "Don't try to distract me."

"Why is this so important to you?"

Luke thought long and hard about his answer. He wanted her to wear the hearing aid to prove that her fears and worst expectations were ungrounded. To show her that he didn't think of her as a deaf woman but as a woman. Mostly, to squelch any comparison between himself and a man who had obviously hurt her with his ignorant insensitivity.

And, if he was honest with himself, he wanted her to agree simply because he had asked her to.

"Will you wear it? For me?" He arched his eyebrows hopefully.

"And you'll sign?" she asked.

"I'll do anything you want me to with my hands."

"You are incorrigible." She pushed her fingers into the silky hair at the base of his neck, urging his head down with gentle pressure. Her lips moved over his mouth.

Jade's sigh of pleasure chimed in unison with the doorbell.

Luke dropped his hand and muttered an expletive.

She giggled. "I caught that, and I'm shocked."

"Right. Like there's a big difference when you say that in sign language. Who would call at such an indecent hour of the morning anyway?"

"You mean, besides yourself?" She stood. "I better get changed while you answer the door. If people are going to think I did something, I'd at least like to be guilty first."

"All right." He came to his feet. "But we'll continue this later."

Luke watched her sprint down the long corridor wearing his baggy sweatshirt. She could exit a room with as much grace and presence as she entered. He glanced at his watch and cursed the timing of the unexpected caller. He went to answer the door.

Kyle's bright face greeted him. His jaw dropped. His sister had not been to his apartment in over five years. He always went to the family house for holidays and visits.

"How did you get here?" He glanced over her shoulder to see if his mother or Robert had also come.

"May I come in?" she signed.

He nodded his head and stepped back to allow her to enter. "Sorry," he gestured.

She shrugged. "I drive now. I *am* eighteen." She frowned, looking a little less sure of her welcome than she had seconds earlier. "Bad time?"

Luke glanced in the direction of the bedroom. "No," he lied.

"You have a girl here!" Her animated features reflected shock.

"Not a *girl*."

"Excuse me. Woman." She waved a finger in his face. "Did I interrupt something? Should I go?"

That was a loaded question. How could he allow her to leave when this was the first time she had visited him on her own?

"No. Don't go," he signed, and walked with her to the living room.

"You're getting good," she noted with her hands. "Your signing."

"Thanks. I'm trying."

She flopped into a chair and folded her legs up under her. "Tell me about this woman."

Luke rolled his eyes and groaned.

* * *

Jade paused in the hall. As she smoothed the wrinkles from her skirt, she wished she had taken a moment to hang the garment last evening. She raked her fingers through the tangled mass of curls and gave up on the idea of restoring order to her hair. Her appearance would have to suffice. She glanced into the living room. Luke was leaning forward in a chair, struggling with Sign Language. Either he took his agreement to sign all day literally or Kyle was the visitor. Although she wished for the former, she feared the latter. Would Kyle be upset about her relationship with Luke? Had Luke even considered the possibility?

Inhaling a deep breath for courage, she walked into the room. ''Good morning,'' she signed.

Kyle's changing expression mirrored her shock as well as her disapproval. For several awkward seconds she just stared. Her eyes filled with tears. She sprung to her feet and bolted for the door.

Luke turned to Jade in numbed surprise. ''What's wrong with her? We were having a pleasant conversation.''

''If you have to ask you wouldn't understand. I'd better go after her.''

Luke came to his feet. ''I'll go.''

''No. You stay here.'' She couldn't find her shoes, so she ran out of the apartment in her bare feet.

Kyle was waiting for the elevator. When she sensed Jade's presence she pushed her finger furiously against the button.

Jade placed a hand on Kyle's arm, but the girl jerked violently away from her. Her icy stare chilled Jade.

"I'm sorry you found out this way."

"But you're not sorry you're sleeping with my brother, right?" Kyle signed furiously.

Jade expected anger but the blunt, untrue accusation about her relationship with Luke still threw her off-balance. "That's really not your business."

"Nothing about Luke is my business. He doesn't want me in his life."

A knot tightened in her stomach. "That's not true. He loves you."

"Sure. That's why he never bothered to learn how to talk with me."

"He's learning now."

Kyle shook her head. "Not for me. For you. Impress the deaf girl with a few tricks. A definite ticket to the bedroom. Any hearing guy will tell you it works every time."

"Luke didn't learn signing for me."

"And I suppose you're not wearing the hearing aid for him, either."

Jade reflexively pulled her hair over her ear. "I understand you're upset."

"Upset? I couldn't care less." Holding her head high, she exhaled a calming breath. "I would expect as much from Luke but I always thought you were smarter than that."

The elevator door swung open. Jade blocked Kyle's path. "Don't leave like this."

"Go back to Luke and leave me alone."

"Kyle . . ."

"You're not my teacher anymore. I don't have to listen to you. I'm going home."

Jade had no choice but to allow Kyle to leave. She was eighteen years old now, not a student who was accountable to her teacher. As the doors slid shut, Jade felt her heart descending with the elevator. She returned to the apartment just as Luke was about to come after her.

"Where's Kyle?" he asked.

"She went home."

"Why is she angry with me?"

"She's not. She's mad at me." Jade pressed her fingers to her temples, trying to ward off the start of a tension headache.

"What for?"

"She's jealous."

"Why?"

"She thought she had finally found her brother, and I took him away."

Luke's mouth curved down in a frown. "Am I supposed to understand this? I thought she'd be happy."

She leaned against the wall and folded her arms across her chest. "Oh, why is that?"

"You have a lot in common."

"Meaning we're both deaf. You figured we'd be playmates or something?"

Fury turned his eyes as dark as onyx. "That's not fair and it's not true."

"I know, and I'm sorry." She wrinkled her nose. It wasn't right to transfer her guilt to Luke. "But the reason you asked me to teach you signing was to improve your relationship with Kyle. If our relationship is going to make matters worse—"

He waved his hand to cut her off. "Don't finish that. She was a little surprised but she'll get over it."

"Do you know your sister well enough to make that claim?" His idea of a "little surprised" might be a major disappointment to Kyle.

"I'll talk to her tomorrow when she's had time to cool off. She'll come around. You'll see."

Jade didn't share his confidence. She recognized misplaced anger. That same sense of hurt she had felt when Anton had ignored her and given his full attention to Luke. But Jade knew how to deal with her feelings. Although technically an adult, Kyle was still immature in many ways and she didn't always channel her anger in a constructive manner.

"I have to go home."

As she turned to leave, he caught her around the waist. "What about this evening?"

A dinner party was the last place she wanted to go. Particularly a business affair. However, she had promised Luke she would attend. "I can't go like this."

"You look fine to me."

"Well, I don't feel fine. I need to put on my battle armor before I go off to the war zone."

"It won't be that bad."

"That remains to be seen." The morning had already been ruined. Her only consolation was that she held no expectations for the rest of the day.

If there was one thing Luke hated, it was being proven wrong. He gazed around the banquet hall with a growing sense of disdain. Too late, he regretted his insistence that Jade wear her hearing aid. She may not have been disappointed by human nature, but his faith in his friends and colleagues had been shaken.

He had spent most of the evening moving Jade out of the line of impolite stares and tactless questions. While she cordially answered direct queries, Luke found himself unable to be so gracious.

"It must be so rewarding working with handicapped children." Alison Taylor's raised voice carried above the murmurs of conversation. The platinum blond had cornered Jade before he could make his way around the table to rescue her.

Jade smiled and shook her head. "My students aren't children and they're not handicapped. They're deaf, like me."

"I never meant to imply that you were handicapped," Alison sputtered. "I apologize if you took it that way."

"No offense taken," Jade said with more politeness than the woman deserved.

"Have you always been deaf?"

Luke groaned. What made that woman think she had a right to delve into Jade's private business? He slipped his arm around her waist. "Let's go."

"Excuse me." Jade shrugged an apology to Alison. The pressure of his hand at the small of her back propelled her forward though the crowded room. As they moved away from the thick of the mob she turned to look at him. "What's wrong this time?"

"We're going."

"The dancing is about to start."

"The perfect time to leave."

The band began to play as they reached the exit doors. He handed his valet parking ticket to a young man, then waited in silence for his car. Jade stood rigid and tense. An overhead spotlight cast a shimmering beam on her ivory satin cocktail dress. Despite the warm summer night, she shivered.

"Your house or mine?" Luke asked when they were settled in the car.

Jade glared at him. "I want to go home."

She was angry, and she had every right to be. He should have listened when she had warned him how people would react.

Minutes later, when they arrived at the condo, she went to her bedroom to change. Luke removed his suit jacket and loosened the tie at his neck.

Jade returned to the living room, dressed in a pair of worn jeans and a tie-dyed sweatshirt. She removed the comb of silk flowers that held her hair in place and set it on the counter. Her hearing aid followed. "The evening is over. I lived up to my end of the bargain."

"I'm sorry about tonight." He reached for her but she backed away.

"Why?"

He tossed his hands up in the air. "You were right. Is that what you wanted to hear?"

She placed her hands on her hips. "What was I right about?"

"That people would treat you like you were handicapped if you wore the hearing aid."

"The only person who treated me like I was handicapped tonight was you."

Luke was stunned by the fiery resentment in her accusation. He had spent most of his time shielding her. "What are you talking about?"

"You answered nearly every question directed at me."

"They were rude questions."

"They were curious inquiries. If you had showed up with a cast on your leg, don't you think people would have asked you what happened?"

He shook his head. "It's not the same thing."

"Yes it is. Why did you insist I wear the hearing aid if all you wanted was a mannequin on your arm?"

"That's not true."

"Then why didn't you let me talk for myself?" Her breath came in short shallow pants.

Luke couldn't understand why she had turned her fury on him. "I was trying to protect you."

"From what?"

"From being hurt."

"You're the one who hurt me." Her eyes shone with unspent tears. "You invited me to a dinner dance, yet you didn't ask me to dance. You wouldn't let me finish a conversation with anyone. And worst of all, you promised to sign, but you didn't try even once."

"You should have reminded me."

"You didn't seem able to forget I was deaf tonight. Why couldn't you remember to sign?"

"I think you're overreacting."

"Well, here's another overreaction. I'd like you to leave. I want to be alone."

"We should talk about this." He cupped his hand on her shoulder.

As he drew her closer, she wedged her arms in between them. "No."

"If you'd just relax. . . ."

"I know." She raked a handful of curls away from her face and sighed. "And then I'd be right in the middle of a relationship that couldn't survive. Thanks, but no thanks."

"You seem to think I was self-conscious about being with you tonight."

"No, Luke. Your actions made *me* feel self-conscious and I don't like to feel that way."

"Jade . . ."

"Would you please leave?" Her barely whispered words contained more warning than if she had shouted. She sidestepped him and walked to her room, slamming the door behind her.

Luke stood alone in utter confusion. He still couldn't figure out what he'd done wrong. Was there a crime in trying to shelter the woman he loved . . . ?

The woman he loved. The idea numbed him with shock. Was this love? This twisting knot in his gut that turned a normally rational man into a social and emotional idiot? If so, he had certainly messed up royally.

Jade watched from the bedroom window until the black sedan pulled away. Her heart ached. She couldn't win. Determined to learn from the mistakes of her engagement, she had chosen not to wear her hearing aid in public. When Luke had insisted, she had allowed herself to hope he might be different.

His actions, although the exact opposite of her ex-fiancé's, had been no less insulting. Did he think she would thank him for leading her around like a child who should be seen and not heard? He should have left her at home.

Why hadn't she followed her instincts? She had questioned the wisdom of becoming involved with

Luke more than once. Kyle's reaction this morning added to Jade's doubt. Tonight only verified her fears. How could she have been so foolish as to fall in love with him?

Jade glanced at the packet of medical forms on her desk. She had procrastinated over filling out the papers and making the appointment. Why? She had the money. She had the time. When had she lost her nerve?

Her thoughts returned to Luke. She had lost her nerve when she had begun to place too much of her future happiness on the outcome. Before she would be ready for the surgery, she had to come to some kind of understanding with Luke about their relationship. Otherwise, she might not be able to handle the very real possibility that the procedure would fail.

Chapter Twelve

The following morning, after a good night's sleep, Luke wasn't any closer to understanding the female psyche. At times like these he knew why he preferred to deal with a computer. Before trying to see Jade again, he figured he'd better straighten out the misunderstanding with his sister.

He walked in the house at precisely ten o'clock in the morning. The chimes of a grandfather clock greeted him. He followed the aroma of fresh coffee to the kitchen. With luck, he had arrived before, not after, breakfast.

As he passed the dining room he noticed Robert propping his head up with one hand and staring into a coffee mug.

"Tough night?" Luke asked.

Robert shrugged. "No worse than any other. How about you? How did your date go?"

"Don't ask."

"That good?" He chuckled. "What happened?"

Luke dropped himself into a chair with a groan.

145

"You might say I tried to put Jade into one of those tiny compartments, as you call them."

"I guess she didn't take it well."

"No. She told me to take a hike."

"I hate to say I told you so."

"Then don't." A stern glare let his cousin know he was in no mood for a lecture. "Is Kyle still sleeping?"

"No. She stayed over at a friend's house last night."

"Which friend?"

"I didn't ask."

Luke grabbed a cup from the china cabinet and poured himself some coffee. He took a large gulp and grunted as he swallowed the cold, bitter brew.

"It's from last night," Robert said. "The fresh stuff is in the kitchen."

"Thanks for telling me," Luke grumbled. "Did Kyle say anything to you?"

"About what?"

"Yesterday morning she stopped by for a visit but took off without a word to me when she saw Jade."

"That's odd. Or maybe not. You're not having much luck with women lately."

"And there's a reason!" Luke thundered. "There is absolutely no logic to their thinking. Leave them alone, they feel ignored. Try to help and you're treating them like a child. What do they want?"

"Hey, if I knew the answer to that I'd write a book and make a fortune."

"Then what did I do wrong?"

"It's bad enough you try to run your family's lives. When you act like an overprotective father with Jade she's going to take it as an insult to her abilities as well as her disabilities."

"The only person who treated me like I was handicapped tonight was you."

So, maybe he had gone too far. But she had been looking for an excuse to pull away from him. From the beginning she had allowed her past experiences to cloud their relationship. All her talk about "her world" and "his world," as if they came from two different planets.

He made a mistake. An error in judgment. However, he'd always prided himself on his ability to learn from his mistakes and not repeat them. Now, all he had to do was convince Jade.

"Why don't you go talk to her?" Robert said, breaking into Luke's thoughts. "I'll tell Kyle you were looking for her when she gets home."

Jade snatched a pair of jeans from the dryer and twisted herself into the still-hot denim. She should have passed on the pint of double fudge ice cream last night but she had been in desperate need of instant gratification. Anger mixed with guilt as she shrugged into a pink-and-white striped pullover.

The last thing she needed this morning was a call from the T.T.Y. operator translating a message from the local police. She had mentally prepared herself for any stupid thing Anton had done. Instead the call had come on behalf of Kyle. Why hadn't she called her own family?

"Of all the moronic, self-destructive things to do," she grumbled as she shoved her feet into a pair of sandals.

As she searched for her keys, Jade debated about calling Luke. She hadn't bothered to check if he had a teletype phone in his apartment and she didn't want to deliver bad news via an operator. Slipping her bank card and driver's license in her back pocket, she headed out the door.

As she sprinted along the sidewalk toward her car, she saw Luke walking in her direction. Her conflicting thoughts on whether or not to stop off at his apartment and tell him about Kyle seemed to be answered by divine intervention. Fate had delivered him at the perfect moment.

"I guess I arrived at a bad time again," he noted. His shoulders hunched slightly forward as he rested his hands in the pockets of his khaki pants.

"Actually, your timing couldn't have been better. You can drive."

His thick brows furrowed in confusion. "May I ask where?"

"First, the nearest ATM and then the Salisburg police station."

"Something happen with Anton?"

Although her brother would be the logical assumption, Jade wasn't up to breaking the news to him yet. Obviously, Kyle's fool-hearted actions were meant to hurt either her or Luke. Maybe both. As much as she still held some of her own anger toward Luke, she didn't relish the job of telling him the depth of his sister's resentment.

"I'll explain when we get there."

She strapped herself into the passenger seat. The fifteen-minute journey passed in strained silence, even for her.

On the steps of the police station, she grabbed Luke's hand. "I better tell you something first. . . ."

"I'm here for you. Whatever it is, I don't care." The genuine glint of sincerity in his eyes dissipated the last of her anger.

"I hope you still feel that way when I tell you that it's your sister, not my brother, who's waiting to be bailed out."

"What?" His fingers clenched around hers in a steely grip. "What happened?"

"All I know is what the desk sergeant said. Breaking and entering, vandalism, and trespassing." Before he could fly off on a rant, she climbed two steps and stood in front of him. "It sounds worse than it is."

"Why did she call you?"

"I don't know. We couldn't speak directly. The police had to call me via the T.T.Y. operator. Maybe she wanted someone to interpret for her before she gave a statement.''

''Which I couldn't do because I don't sign, right?''

''I didn't say that.'' She pressed her palm into his shoulder. ''What happened to 'I'm here for you. No matter what it is, I don't care'?''

''She shouldn't have involved you.''

''Don't you think she knew I'd call you? This was directed at us, otherwise she would have called Robert to bail her out.''

He lowered his eyes and released her hand. ''You're right.''

''Should we go bail her out?''

''I guess so. I'll pay you back at home.''

''No. She will.''

While Jade spoke with Kyle and the arresting police officer, Luke had a talk with the owner of the building that his sister had targeted for her folly. He agreed with the unsympathetic gentleman that acts of vandalism should not be tolerated, but Luke still allowed his guilt to rule his head. After agreeing to pay all of the damages, plus a little extra for the man's inconvenience, the charges against Kyle were dropped.

The air in the car during the ride home was as thick as a winter fog and almost as chilly. When Luke pulled into the parking lot of his building, Kyle signed to Jade.

''She wants to go home,'' Jade translated.

He shook his head. ''Too bad. I'm not really concerned with her wants right now.''

Kyle responded to his answer with a cold, indifferent glare. Shoving her hands in the pockets of her scruffy jeans, she stomped her feet across the pavement as they walked to the building. Her actions reminded him of the four-year-old sister who threw tantrums when she didn't get her way. He had excused her behavior then because she had been a child. He had excused her rudeness later because of his own failure to sign. But he could not allow her to hurt herself and the rest of the family when she was mad at him.

Holding Kyle's arm, he guided her to the dining room and pulled out a chair. She flopped down in the seat and put her elbows on the teakwood tabletop. He sat directly across from her.

''Please sit down,'' he signed to Jade.

''Maybe I should leave,'' she returned.

''No!'' he said, then added, ''Please.''

Jade shrugged and took the chair next to Luke.

''What were you thinking?'' he asked his sister.

Kyle pretended not to catch his words. She and Jade began a rapid succession of signs, most of which he couldn't follow. Every so often he saw Jade shake her head or respond with a firm ''no.'' As Kyle grew more animated, her face flushed scarlet, yet Jade never lost her temper. By the looks he received every few seconds, he knew he was the center of the conversation, but he felt no ego boost from the fact.

"No, I won't," Jade said and signed. "No . . . I won't tell him that . . . tell him yourself. . . ."

"Tell me what?" Luke asked.

"Tell him," Kyle signed, smacking her hand against the table for added emphasis. "He doesn't understand the signs."

Jade shifted her gaze between the two siblings. "I won't do it. If you want him to know, then *you* make him understand."

"How?" Kyle asked with her hands.

Jade tilted her head to one side. "You know how."

Luke met Kyle's unwavering stare. His sister seemed to be weighing her options. Suddenly, with a clarity he hadn't quite expected, she spoke the first words he'd heard from her in over five years.

"I hate you."

Jade recoiled as if she'd heard a gunshot, then slumped in the chair and lowered her head. Although Kyle's declaration was directed at him, her words seemed to cut deeply into Jade as well. For him, that made the hurt twice as painful.

"You don't mean that," he said.

"How do you know? You don't know me. You never wanted to." Although she spoke slowly and punctuated her words with angry gestures, his sister had no trouble making her point.

"That's not true," he signed.

"Save your little tricks for Ms. Allenwood. I'm sure she's impressed by them. Or are you going to tell me that she has nothing to do with your sudden interest in learning to sign? Eighteen years of having me as your sister never sparked an interest."

Luke inhaled deeply. He gazed toward Jade, who tried her best not to involve herself in the discussion. "Yes, I am learning because of her . . ."

Kyle let out a bitter laugh. "So, you admit it."

"Because of her. But not *for* her."

"What's the difference?"

"I don't have to sign to communicate with her. She doesn't ignore me if I talk."

"Well, she should."

He nodded. "Maybe she should. But she makes allowances for my faults. That's what people do when they care about other people. They make allowances."

"At least you recognize your faults."

"If I hadn't known I'd made a mistake, I wouldn't be trying to rectify it. I guess the question is, should I continue to try?"

She shrugged as if she didn't care. "That's up to you."

"No. It's up to you. If you don't want me in your life, say so. Because your actions today, as much as they were designed to spite me, would hurt Mother if she knew."

A flash of sorrow crossed her face. "You're not going to tell her?"

"No. You tell her if you want."

"Not right now," Kyle mumbled, looking repentant. "I should call her. I'm supposed to be at my friend's house."

"The Teletype phone is in the study."

"I know. I used to come here a lot."

"Quite often, I remember." As a child, she had loved to visit his apartment because he had let her do whatever she wanted. Back then they hadn't needed to communicate with words or Sign. A simple touch or a swing up to his shoulders had been enough. The long span of silent years between then and now might be more than the memories could bridge.

Jade remained silent, feeling partly responsible. She hadn't expected Kyle to express herself in such a cruel manner. Jade's annoyance with Luke had all but dissolved, replaced with an ache of sympathy. She wiped the back of her hand across her damp cheek and sucked in a calming breath.

His fingers laced through hers. A warm sensation of comfort pulsed through her. She glanced up.

"Are you okay?" he asked.

"Yeah. How about you?"

"What am I supposed to do with her?"

"Give her a job?" she suggested.

"Oh, right. She hates me. Do you really think she's going to work for me?"

She frowned. Luke didn't understand his sister at

all. "She doesn't hate you, she wanted to get your attention."

"Well, she succeeded, big time."

"Then stop treating her like your invalid baby sister, incapable of taking care of herself, and make her take responsibility for her actions."

"By putting her to work?"

"Who is going to pay for the damage she did?"

"You might be right there."

"I know I am." She rose and stepped around the table. Luke followed. "I should be shoving off."

"Not yet." He cupped his hands over the indentation of her waist. "I wanted to talk to you about last night."

She fought the desire to lose herself in the woodsy smell of him, to drown in the warm brown eyes that implored her to stay. "Later. You have a lot of things to straighten out with Kyle."

"How are you going to get home?"

"I'll take a cab."

"Take my car. I'll catch a ride to your place later."

Behind his generous offer, she saw his ulterior motive. If he had to pick up his car, she would have to be home for him later. By accepting his keys, she would cede control to him once again. Was she destined to repeat her own painful history?

"I'll see you." She took the gold key ring from his hand and slid it in her pocket. As he lowered his head, she turned to receive his kiss on her cheek. "It won't be that easy, Luke."

"I never thought it would."

"Tell Kyle I said . . ." She made the sign for good-bye and, with a backward wave, she left the apartment.

She took the long route back to her condo. The supple leather and overloaded gadgets in his Mercedes were a striking contrast to her stripped-down model. She took the opportunity to test drive the luxury car. Besides, driving always relaxed her, and she was feeling tense. She had a few major decisions to make about the direction of her life, and so far she had successfully managed to avoid making even one.

She believed every word she said to Luke about making his sister take personal responsibility for her actions. Why had she never applied her good advice to herself in regard to Anton? Why had she accepted the brunt of his guilt and anger, yet denied her own?

When she finally pulled the car up in front of her condo, she saw her brother sitting on the wrought-iron bench on her porch. She wasn't surprised, as if some sixth sense had told her he would be here today. And if her psychic senses were anything to judge by, this was not going to be a pleasant visit.

Chapter Thirteen

Anton rose as she walked up the sidewalk. His chinos and cotton sport shirt were wrinkled, as if he had slept in his clothes. Taking in the dark circles under his eyes and his tousled hair, she figured he hadn't been home last night. Or maybe he didn't have a home any longer.

"It's about time," he said.

"I'm sorry. Did we have plans today?" Her sarcasm was lost on Anton. She unlocked the door.

With a nervous glance over his shoulder, he pushed his way in front of her and stepped inside.

"Won't you come in, Anton," she sniped to his back.

He turned and nodded. "Sorry. How are you?"

"Fine."

Anton peered out the window then closed the vertical blinds. He was more anxious than normal, almost frightened.

"This isn't a social call, is it?" she asked.

"Is your boyfriend around?"

"My boyfriend?"

"Luke."

She shook her head and exhaled a groan. "No. But if you wanted to see him, I'll give you his address."

"That's not what I meant. I never say the right thing when I talk to you."

"The right thing?" she repeated. "Why not try the truth?"

"I'm in trouble."

"What kind of trouble?"

"I owe this guy some money . . ."

Jade rolled her eyes and let out an exaggerated sigh. "There's a surprise. Did you ever think about getting a job?"

He balled his fingers into fists. "I don't have time."

"What do you do all day?"

"I don't have time to make the kind of money I need."

"How bad off are you?"

"Fifteen grand."

She swallowed a choked cough. "Fifteen thousand dollars? How did you get yourself in that deep?"

"Does it matter?"

"I guess not."

"Do you have the money or not?" he asked pointedly.

"Can't you pay it off in installments?"

He glanced at her as if she were crazy. "This is not a loan to a credit union, Isabella."

"So if you can't pay, what happens? They break your legs?"

"If I'm lucky, that's all they'll do." Anton's flair for theatrics stopped her from taking him seriously.

"Don't you think you're being over dramatic?"

"Not this time."

Jade sank into the recliner. "What makes you think I have that kind of money?"

"You have the condo. You must have some equity in the place."

"You expect me to borrow against my home?" His sheer audacity surprised her, and she had thought she was immune to shock from her brother.

"I'll pay you back."

"When, Anton? When? You've never paid me back a dime in your life." Salty tears pooled in her eyes. She inhaled a large, calming breath and exhaled slowly. She would not cry.

Anton squatted down by the arm of the chair and locked an imploring gaze on her. "Please, Isabella. This is serious. If I don't pay up in three days this guy is gonna rearrange my organs. Can you help me or not?"

"Yes." Her heart answered before her mind had time to consider the consequences. If helping family was supposed to be a rewarding experience, why did she feel this vast emptiness?

"Can I get the money tomorrow?"

"Tomorrow is a bank holiday. Fourth of July. It will have to be Tuesday."

"Thanks, thanks." The lines of tension around his face relaxed slightly. He stood. "I'd better take off."

"Good idea." She walked Anton to the door.

"I'll meet you at the bank on Tuesday. Nine o'clock?" he said.

"I work. You'll have to meet me on my lunch hour. One o'clock." She caught his arm to halt his normally speedy exit. "One more thing, Anton."

"What?"

A chilling numbness washed over her. Giving up on a person never came easy to her, but she hadn't done her brother any service by always bailing him out of trouble. "After you get the money, I don't ever want to see you again. If you get yourself in trouble don't come to me."

He slid his hands in his pockets and hunched his shoulders. "I understand your anger."

"I don't care if you understand it. I deserve better than I've gotten from you."

"Because I was responsible for you losing your hearing."

"You've played that card for the last time. I'm through feeling guilty about you feeling guilty. From now on, just leave me alone."

After Anton left, Jade walked around the condo, restlessly straightening the bric-a-brac on the shelves. Fifteen thousand dollars! Even if she continued with her life-style of scrimping and saving and taking second jobs, this would set her back eight to ten months.

Gooseflesh covered her arms. Her stomach knotted. She might not have made her decision about the surgery, but now she no longer had a choice. At least not any time soon.

She picked up a photograph of herself and Anton, snapped at a science fair a month before her accident. It was the last picture taken of them together. Anton held up his Junior Chemistry award and grinned like a Cheshire cat. He'd had such potential.

"What a waste!" she cried as she flung the picture frame into the wall. Glass shattered on the kitchen counter and floor.

She stared at the mess, unable to believe her own violent action. From the remnants of splintered wood and glass she removed two pieces of the photograph than had severed in half. The cut fell right between the two siblings.

Luke heard the loud crash as he walked up the sidewalk to Jade's condo. His anxiety rose. He rapped his knuckles on the door twice, waited, then knocked again. Why didn't she answer? He glanced at the small gold-lettered sign that read PLEASE RING BELL. He could knock until he bruised his hand but unless she had the hearing aid in, she wouldn't hear him. Once again, his brain had ceased to function. He pushed the button.

Seconds later, Jade pulled the door open. Wet streaks stained her face. She started to say something but the angry outburst died on her lips.

"Are you okay?" He took hold of her arm and led her toward the sofa. "Sit down."

"I have to clean up a mess first," she muttered, easing her arm away from him.

"An accident?"

"Yeah. I threw a picture frame at the wall and it accidently broke."

"Were you thinking about me when you threw it?"

A tiny laugh mingled with a hiccup. "Not this time. Your keys are on the hall table."

"Are you kicking me out?"

"You might be safer. No telling what might come flying at your head if I don't like what you're saying." She bent down to pick up the pieces of glass. Her hair fell in a tousled mass of ringlets around her face. As his gaze traveled lower, he noted how her worn denim jeans molded her long legs.

Before his thoughts led him into trouble, he crouched down to help her. Taking the dust pan and brush from her, he swept up the small splinters of the broken frame.

"I'll get the rest with the vacuum," she said.

Her hand trembled. Earlier at the police station and then at his apartment, she had been in complete control. What had happened in the last few hours? He wanted to erase the sadness etched into her face but she moved away before he could reach for her.

When he stood up again, he noticed the torn photograph on the counter. Relief ran through him. Now he knew who was behind her radical mood swing, and thankfully, he wasn't the cause this time.

As Jade ran the electric sweeper over the carpet and kitchen floor, her angry, jerking movements seemed gradually to relax. By the time she finished, her emotions were back under control.

"How's Kyle?" she asked. She held up a ceramic mug. "Coffee?"

He nodded and sat on a stool at the counter. "She's still ticked off at me but she seems to be excited about working at the office."

"Well, sure. It's the first thing you've done that shows her you are treating her like a *normal* adult."

"Was her stunt last night meant to prove that to me?"

"She got through to you, didn't she?"

He shrugged a reluctant agreement. "Does that mean she's gonna lighten up on the signing and talk to me sometimes?"

"Don't count on it. She's been deaf her entire life so she's likely to be more insistent about that issue than I am." Jade poured a cup of coffee and slid it across the counter to him. "You're the only member of your family who doesn't sign. I'm the only member of my family who does. Kyle and I tend to see this from a different perspective.''

''Does that mean you're gonna lighten up on me?''

''Probably,'' she said sadly.

''Don't make it sound like a tragedy.''

''From my point of view, it is.''

Luke took a sip of his coffee. So, she was still upset about their less-than-perfect date last evening. Although they had a lot to talk about regarding his tendency to overprotect, Jade had residual anger toward her brother and he didn't want to share that blame. He had enough explaining of his own to do.

He rested his elbows on the butcher block counter. ''What did Anton want?''

''How did you know he was here?''

''I know everything about you.''

She rolled her eyes. ''I guess you saw him leave.''

''Actually, I figured that's why you hurled his picture at the wall.''

''Maybe I didn't have one of you.''

''I'm right here. Shove me into the wall if you want.''

''Don't tempt me.'' She scooted around the counter and walked into the living room.

As she passed him, he caught her by the waistband of her jeans. She stumbled backward against his chest. Before she could twist free, he slipped his hands over her waist from behind and locked her between his upper arms. Using his free hands he signed, "I am talking to you."

For a few confusing moments Jade remained sheltered in the warmth and strength of Luke's body. A jumble of emotions ran through her and she wasn't sure where to focus her feelings. On Luke, who could so easily make her forget how hard she had fought to reach a point in her life where she relied on no one? Or did she concentrate on Anton, who in a ten-minute visit had managed to destroy a two-year dream?

Blaming anyone but herself was too convenient. She had allowed Anton to ruin her plans because she was scared. Without the money, she couldn't give the new surgical procedure a try. If she didn't try, it couldn't fail.

Luke turned her in the circle of his arms. He kissed her tenderly, the gentle caress of his lips reminding her that despite his faults, he touched her in a way no other person could. Was it enough to base an entire relationship on when they had nothing else in common?

"Are you going to tell me about your brother's visit?"

"What's to tell? He wanted money, but there's nothing new about that."

"If it's not unusual, why were you upset?"

"He doesn't normally ask for fifteen thousand dollars."

Luke's eyes widened. "That's a lot of milk money. What about his job?"

"If he's working, it's news to me. He hasn't held a steady job in his life."

"Then say no."

If only she could. "He claims he owes a loan shark. How do I live with myself if something happens to him?"

He stroked his hand over her shoulder. "Do you have the money?"

After a long pause she answered, "Yes."

"But you were saving that for surgery."

Her jaw dropped open. She'd never told anyone about her plans. Either Luke read minds or she talked in her sleep. "How did you know?"

"The magazines on the coffee table gave me a clue. And a few things you've said. I guess insurance doesn't cover the cost."

She never realized that he paid such close attention to details. Or maybe she hadn't paid attention herself. "No. And the hospital wants the money up front."

"If it's only a matter of money, I'll give—"

"No!"

"I'll lend—"

"Still no."

"Why?"

The corners of her mouth lifted in a sad smile. "I appreciate the offer, but I don't borrow money. That way I don't owe anyone."

"Even me?"

"Especially you. You try to run my life as it is. Heaven help me if I owed you money."

"Then before we talk about the money let's straighten out what happened last night."

"Forget it."

"No. You brought up the subject. I'm sorry about the way I reacted. I should have known better."

She wriggled against him, trying to free herself. He tightened his grip so that her twisting only served to make her completely aware of every inch of his well-toned body. "It's over."

"It's not over, Jade. Because I still think you should wear the hearing aid when you go out. And if I made you more self-conscious about that, I'm really sorry."

"It's all right."

"It's not all right."

"Don't you know how to let something drop? You're forgiven. What does it take to convince you?"

"Another chance? We'll go out again, and this time I will sign if I have to tape a note onto my tuxedo lapel to remind myself. I won't cut off your conversations."

"And you'll dance with me?"

"No."

"Why?" she asked.

"I can't dance."

"Oh, baloney. Anyone can dance."

His forehead creased in confusion. "And there's a point to it?"

"That depends on who your partner is." She pressed in closer.

He expelled a heavy breath. "I guess I am forgiven."

"Forgiven, yes. But how much further we can go with our relationship remains to be seen. You haven't met any of my friends yet. You might not feel any more comfortable in my world than you made me feel in yours."

"I am capable of compromise. I've just never had much practice. I'm used to being in control, but that doesn't mean I can't change."

He seemed genuinely sincere. At least he was willing to try, which gave her encouragement. "Okay, Mr. Clayborne. We'll give it another shot."

His half smile was either one of relief or triumph, and right now, she really didn't want to know which. She might have made the biggest mistake of her life and all she could think about was how much she needed him in her life. Under any circumstances, on any terms.

There was always a danger in wanting something or someone too much. Against her own better judgment she had lost a piece of herself to Luke. She wouldn't have minded if she thought she had gotten a piece of him back in return.

Chapter Fourteen

Jade dropped her purse inside the desk drawer and flipped on the switch for her computer. Before beginning her work, she took a moment to thumb through the fall catalog that Direct Mail had released. She thought about asking Luke for an employee discount, but she knew that he would refuse to let her pay any part of an order.

After marking a few pages for later consideration, she put the catalog aside. Remembering that she had a lunchtime meeting with Anton at the bank, she decided against any impulse purchasing. Her stomach muscles contracted and the anxiety she had put out of her mind the past two days returned.

She had spent Independence Day with Luke, for the most part, cuddled up against him. When she felt ambitious she moved as far as the kitchen. Luke had managed to keep her mind off Anton, but very little else between them had been settled. Except for one issue. She absently smoothed her hair over her hearing aid.

Although she preferred the kind of diversion that Luke offered, work was another way to keep her thoughts off her problems. She started to keypunch the first batch of orders. As she worked, she blocked out the carryings-on around her. The muffled sound of a cough broke her focus about halfway through the stack. She swiveled in her chair.

Kyle sent her an uncertain smile and signed, "Hello."

"Hi."

With her crisp white blouse tucked into a pair of powder blue slacks and her hair neatly fastened in a barrette, Kyle looked older than her eighteen years. "Luke thought you would be the best person to train me."

"You're starting in Data Entry?"

"I wanted to be the boss but Luke's attached to that job."

Jade frowned. "Is this a big joke to you?"

"No." Kyle shook her head. "I guess you're still mad at me."

Two coworkers watched their exchange with obvious interest. Normally she wouldn't mind, but whether signing or speaking, it was a private conversation. She waved to the women and, seemingly embarrassed by their rude stares, they returned to their work.

"Why would I be mad?" Jade gestured. "You didn't do anything to me."

"I was a total witch when I found out about you and Luke."

She tipped her head. "I understood. You thought I was taking your brother away."

"No. I didn't want my brother taking you away. You were my favorite teacher. The way you always stood up for me, always defended me. You were one of us."

Jade felt a sorrowful ache around her heart. "I'm still the same person."

"You don't communicate with speech at school."

"Of course not, because all my students and colleagues sign. But away from work, I do both depending on who I'm with. And if you'll recall, I've always been in favor of my students learning both ways to communicate."

"I know. I just felt that you were defending Luke instead of me." Kyle's honest and insightful admission caught Jade by surprise.

"Maybe just because he needs it more right now." She winked and Kyle nodded her agreement. "Should we get started? You wouldn't want the boss to think you're goofing off on your first day. Makes a bad impression, you know."

"Like he doesn't expect it."

"Then prove him wrong." Jade picked up a stack of order forms and removed the rubber band. Pointing toward an empty chair, she waited for Kyle to position herself in front of the computer before starting.

"So, are you and Luke serious?"

Jade ignored the question. "The first thing you do

is enter the catalog key number. It's highlighted on the form in yellow.''

"You were with him yesterday. I tried to call but he was out all day.''

"Next you enter the customer account number. If they don't have an account, you set one up using their zip code and the first three numbers of the billing address.''

"And half the night,'' Kyle signed.

"What are we discussing?''

"Luke. He must have gotten home very late last night.''

Jade drummed her fingers against the desk. "Are we going to teach you how to enter orders?''

"Robert taught me yesterday so I would be prepared. It's easy.''

"Then why are you sitting with me?''

"I'm trying to find out about you and my brother.''

Jade felt a warm flush creep up her cheeks. "Go ask him.''

"I did. He told me to come out here and sit with you.''

"He meant to work.''

Kyle shrugged in defeat. "All right. Point me in the direction of a free desk and I'll work. We can continue this conversation at lunch.''

"Not today,'' Jade signed. "I have plans.'' She would prefer a grilling from Luke's sister to the meeting with her brother.

Throughout the morning Jade's apprehension grew. By the time her lunch hour arrived, she had a full-blown anxiety attack. What if Anton didn't show? Would she be relieved or more worried? She tried to see Luke before she left, hoping the sight of him, so calm, so contained, would rub off on her. But he was out of the office.

The twenty-minute cab ride to the bank did little to relax her. She arrived at ten minutes past one o'clock and Anton was nowhere to be seen. For five minutes she nervously paced the bank lobby until she was sure the security guard thought she was casing the joint. She was about to leave when Anton walked in the door.

His carefree grin stung like vinegar on an open wound. "Sorry I'm late."

"Let's just get this over with," she snapped. As she started to walk toward the window, he grabbed her arm.

"Isabella." She stopped and fixed her gaze on him. "I don't need the money. I would have called to save you the trip but . . ."

"You don't need it?" she repeated incredulously. "Three days ago you told me some guy was going to break your legs. What's going on?"

"I had a lucky streak."

"Are you telling me that while you were fifteen thousand dollars in debt you were trying to gamble your way out?'' A shudder of anger ripped through her.

"Not exactly."

"You hit the lottery, perhaps?" she grumbled in distaste.

He raked a hand through his meticulously styled hair. "I figured you'd be relieved that I didn't need the money."

"Not if I have to worry about where you got it."

"Does it matter, Isabella?"

"I'm beginning to think it does."

"Why?"

"Because you're refusing to answer." She folded her arms across her chest. "Did you call Mom?"

"No."

"Because she can't afford to send you what little she does have."

"I said I didn't go to Mom."

"I'll have to take your word." She wouldn't know if her brother had a friend capable of raising that kind of money. Had he conned some unsuspecting woman? Her mind raced with possibilities. "You didn't go to Luke, did you?"

Stupid question. How would Anton know how to contact Luke? She noted the expression of shock on her brother's face. Maybe it wasn't such a stupid question. "You're not borrowing the money from Luke, are you?"

"I didn't call him."

Jade picked up on the careful wording. "Did he give you the money?"

"Give?"

"Loan?" she corrected.

"What's the difference?"

"For you, none. To me, a big difference."

"Then I suggest you ask him."

"I will."

Without so much as a good-bye, she spun on her heels and stormed out of the bank. She hailed a cab by standing in the center of the road and forcing the driver to stop or run her over. She answered his ranting with a general observation about the male population as she took up position in the back seat. After a few minutes she apologized to the man for taking out her frustrations on him instead of directing her anger where it belonged—with Luke.

Luke returned the phone to the cradle. He had hoped he would have time to tell Jade himself, but he wasn't surprised that she had figured out where Anton got the money on her own. He checked his watch. She should be back in about ten minutes. Just enough time to cancel his afternoon appointments and still get down to the lobby before she returned.

She stepped from the taxi and stormed across the street like a tornado. Her expression was thunderous and became downright volatile when she saw him.

"Should we walk or take the car to a more private

place?'' he asked. Her forehead creased in piqued confusion. ''I assume you don't want any witnesses when you kill me.''

''I have to go back to work.''

''Not this afternoon. We have to talk.''

Her icy glare sent a chill through him. ''You should have talked to me before you went to see Anton. I told you I didn't want to borrow your money.''

He took her elbow and led her toward his car. ''I didn't lend you any.''

''You gave it to Anton.''

''And that's between him and me.''

''I'll write you a check.''

''I won't accept it.'' He unlocked the passenger side door and motioned for her to get in. She stood her ground firmly for a few tense seconds, then slid in and fastened the seat belt with a groan. During the short ride to her condo, she kept her fingers clenched tightly into fists. He thought better of trying to talk to her until the car came to a final halt.

She bolted to her front door before he even cut the engine. As he came up behind her, she whirled around and grabbed his suit jacket by the lapels. ''You had no right to go behind my back. When are you going to get out of my problems?''

''When you get out of my heart.''

She shook her head as if she hadn't understood his words. ''What?''

''I have no intention of butting out of your life.

When you're upset, I can't think. I can't concentrate on work and I can't eat. It's darned unhealthy for me.''

"This isn't about you."

He tossed his hands in the air. "I'm a self-centered egotist. Everything is about me."

"That's not funny, Luke."

"It's not?" he asked.

She pushed him back as she let him go. "Stop it."

"Stop what?"

"Don't you realize you'll never see that money again?" She fumbled with her keychain.

He took the keys and opened the front door. "I don't expect to. I expect to see his sorry self at the warehouse for the next six months."

Her eyes rounded into two gleaming emeralds. "You gave him a job?"

"Someone's going to pay me back that money. I figured he was the logical choice."

"And you think he's going to show up?" She gazed at him as if he were a few bricks short of a full load.

"He's more likely to pay me back than you. It's a male thing. You wouldn't understand."

"Try me."

"I threatened to rearrange his organs myself if he doesn't."

Her eyebrow arched in question. "And he was worried?"

"I can be very convincing when I want to be."

Jade leaned her back against the counter and knotted her fingers together. "I'll grant you that."

He stood in front of her and traced a finger over her arm. "Then why can't I convince you that our relationship can work?"

She was still fuming mad at him and he wanted to discuss the future? He couldn't respect her wishes in the present. "This isn't the right time or place for that."

"When and where?"

"Excuse me?"

"Name the time and place and I'll be there."

She grabbed hold of his hand before his featherlike stroking drove her to distraction. Luke was too adept at diverting her attention. "This isn't about us. It's about you giving money to Anton."

"Yes, I gave it to him. And I'd do it again."

"You have to stop interfering in my life."

"Why?"

"I'm not an invalid. I can take care of myself."

"I never doubted that for a moment. I don't do things because I think you can't, but because it's the only way I know. I'll admit that sometimes I'm a bit overprotective, even controlling. . . ."

"Try pushy, manipulative, and overbearing."

His mouth curved down in a frown. "Maybe I go too far occasionally. However, I'm not unreasonable. I'd listen if you would talk to me instead of getting all defensive about how you can take care of your-self.''

''We're getting away from the point, Luke.''

''You want to stick to the point? The money is an excuse. Just like the surgery is an excuse and the 'deaf culture' is an excuse. You use them to push me away because you're scared. You got hurt once and you're afraid I'm going to hurt you, too.''

''Where did you come up with that brilliant theory, Einstein?''

''Oh, come on. You've been running since the first day I met you.''

''Running? Because I choose to handle my own problems alone? What gave you the right to go against my wishes?''

''I love you.''

''That's not love, Luke.''

''You think not? Do you love me?''

''We're not discussing that . . .''

''Yes or no?''

''Yes.'' He had never given her any choice in that matter. He had stolen her heart from day one and he obviously had no intention of giving it back.

''And is there anything you won't do for someone you love? You were going to give your brother your hard-earned savings. Reverse the situation and tell me with all honesty that you would allow *my* pride to stand in the way of your helping me.''

Upon thought, her answer would have to be a resounding no. She would do anything for Luke, and that was what scared her the most. "It wasn't for me. It was for Anton."

"Family is all part of the deal. Did I get mad when you were going to bail my sister out of jail?"

"You paid off the complainant."

"Only because I arrived when I did. Would you have told me otherwise?"

"Afterward," she admitted somewhat reluctantly. Oh, she hated that he was right.

"And I planned to tell you about your brother. Afterward."

"After what?"

He grinned sheepishly. "Preferably after we were married a few years."

"That's what I thought. What makes you think I'd marry you?"

"Would you?"

"I don't know. I'll answer that question if and when it's asked."

"I'm asking," he said simply.

Jade searched his face for a hint of a smile. She kept waiting for the punchline. Since he had declared his love for her in the middle of an argument, she hadn't taken his earlier words seriously. The only emotion she could read in his eyes now was uncertainty.

Luke glanced away. "Say something."

"I don't know what to say," she said, trying hard not to cry. She had never considered the possibility.

He took her into his arms. She was sheltered by his strength, and she liked the feeling. He rested his chin on her shoulder and sprinkled kisses over her neck and face. She had neither the willpower nor the desire to offer resistance.

Luke traced his thumb over her hearing aid. "Can you hear me?"

"Yes."

"Clearly?"

"Pretty much."

"I just want to make sure you hear this. I love you and I want to marry you."

"Why?"

"Because that's what most people do when they're in love. They get married."

She swallowed hard. "We're not like most people."

"I don't think of us as being any different."

Her mind reeled. "I need time to think. Perhaps after the surgery . . ."

"No. I need an answer before."

"Why?"

"Because I don't care about the outcome or if you even decide to have the operation. But if you're not sure about me now, you'll always doubt me if the surgery isn't successful."

In her heart, Jade knew he was right. Her doubts had never been for Luke but for herself. Knowing that he loved her, that he wanted to make a life with her, made all the difference in the way she viewed his interfering, albeit well-intentioned, actions. "You really don't care, one way or the other?"

He gazed at her with the eyes of a man who saw only the best in her. "Not a bit."

"I still don't feel right about you giving Anton that money."

He let out an exasperated groan. "All right. You pay me back the money. After we're married, *we* will pay for the surgery if you decide to give it a try. Would that make you feel better?"

She smiled and slipped her arms around his neck. "Yes."

"You're so stubborn."

"I have to be or you'll ride roughshod over me the rest of our lives."

"Does that mean you will marry me?" Luke seemed to be holding his breath as he waited for an answer.

"Yes, I'll marry you." She tipped her head back and kissed him, fiercely, passionately, until she couldn't catch a breath. After she broke away, she nuzzled her face against his chest and felt his unsteady heartbeat keeping rhythm with her own. This was the music that had been missing from her life. "Did I forget to tell you that I love you too?"

"It may have slipped your mind, but I never doubted it for a minute."

She shook her head. "After we're married I'm going to have to do something about your ego."

"After we're married you can do anything you want with me. As a matter of fact, why don't you start now?"

"I really should get back to work. My boss would be very upset if he knew I had skipped out for an afternoon dalliance."

Luke grinned. "Would you like me to talk to him for you?"

"No. I have to learn how to get around him on my own. I might as well start now." She gazed at his smiling face. They would spend half their marriage locked in a battle of wills. Did she really want to do that to herself?

Absolutely.

Epilogue

Jade sat cross-legged on the hospital bed. Two poinsettias adorned the windowsill. She ran a finger over a rose petal from the large red and green floral arrangement on the bedside table. A papier-mâché Santa wiggled on his wooden stick. That's what she got for scheduling her operation during winter recess.

She enjoyed the moment of solitude while Luke walked his mother and sister back to their car. Although five months of marriage had drastically curbed his tendency to control, the impending surgery had sent him into a temporary relapse. Perhaps his fear was caused by the fact that he couldn't control the outcome, so he had to take charge of everything else in a five-mile radius.

Luke burst through the door. Evidently he had sprinted back from the parking lot at a record-setting pace. "Did you miss me?" he signed.

"More than life itself. I was counting the seconds until your return. All sixty of them."

"Smarty." He joined her on the bed. "Aren't you going to change?"

"Not until they make me." She had passed on the ever-fashionable green-and-white striped hospital gown in favor of one of Luke's T-shirts.

He slid his arm across her shoulders. "Anton wants to visit you tomorrow."

"What did you tell him?"

"He hasn't missed a day of work in nearly six months. Don't you think it's time you let up?"

Luke had been right about her brother. As long as he believed he owed Luke the money, he had not missed a single payment. And as long as Jade stayed angry with Anton, he kept trying to make the past up to her. Had she known that he needed her to blame him for the accident, she would have told him off sooner and they could have gotten on with repairing their relationship.

"Oh, I guess you can tell him it's all right to visit."

"Little liar. You want him to come." He tugged the bedsheet over her legs and tucked the edges. "I'll go call him. And then I have to check on a few things."

She grabbed his arm as he started to rise. "Cut it out."

"What am I doing?"

"Stop telling the nurses and doctors how to do their jobs."

"I don't do that."

She swallowed a laugh. "I need you here with me."

He stroked the back of his hand over her cheek.

"I'm with you, Jade. I'll always be with you no matter what happens."

"I know."

"Do you, or are you just saying that?" Despite the numerous times they'd had this discussion in the past month, he still seemed to think she had doubts about him.

"I don't think I would have come this far if I didn't believe that. But, whether the procedure is successful or not doesn't matter, because I'll still have you. Right?"

He placed his hand on her shoulder and pushed her down into the pillows. "Just try to get rid of me."

"The thought never entered my mind." He was definitely a good thing in her life. No matter what happened, she knew she could count on him.